"Truce?"

Spencer lifted his eyebrows, making me wait for his reply. Was he going to tell me to get lost? Had I blown this job? Had my stupidity gotten in the way?

"You're something else," he said a few heartbeats later. He didn't sound amused. But he didn't sound angry anymore, either. He expelled a breath and added, "But you always were feisty."

I used to be a full-on brat, but I wasn't going to cop to it now. I flashed a hopeful smile. "You're not firing me?"

"I guess not." He glanced at my lips, as if he was remembering the taste of them.

He stood and walked over to the bar. Seconds ticked by, or maybe it was minutes. I wanted to break the silence, but I couldn't think of an intelligible thing to say. I was remembering the taste of his lips, too.

* * *

Hot Nashville Nights by Sheri WhiteFeather
is part of the Daughters of Country series.

Dear Reader,

Music has always been a significant part of my life. From the time I was a child, I didn't just listen to my favorite songs, I was fascinated by the lyrics, hanging on every word.

In this book, *Hot Nashville Nights*, the hero is a highly successful songwriter. His name is Spencer Riggs and his love interest is Alice McKenzie. Some of you might recall Alice from *Nashville Secrets*, my March 2019 Harlequin Desire. She was a secondary character in that story, creating a bit of havoc for her older sister.

Alice is still struggling with issues from the past, and so is Spencer, the troubled songwriter stealing her heart. Together, they are filled with passion, much like the songs Spencer writes.

Love and hugs,

Sheri WhiteFeather

SHERI WHITEFEATHER

HOT NASHVILLE NIGHTS

HARLEQUIN
DESIRE

HARLEQUIN®

DESIRE™

Recycling programs
for this product may
not exist in your area.

ISBN-13: 978-1-335-20916-0

Hot Nashville Nights

Copyright © 2020 by Sheree Henry-Whitefeather

This edition published by arrangement with Harlequin Books S.A.

For questions and comments about the quality of this book,
please contact us at CustomerService@Harlequin.com.

Harlequin Enterprises ULC
22 Adelaide St. West, 40th Floor
Toronto, Ontario M5H 4E3, Canada
www.Harlequin.com

Printed in U.S.A.

Sheri WhiteFeather is an award-winning bestselling author. She lives in Southern California and enjoys shopping in vintage stores and visiting art galleries and museums. She is known for incorporating Native American elements into her books and has two grown children who are tribally enrolled members of the Muscogee Creek Nation. Visit her website at www.sheriwhitefeather.com.

Books by Sheri WhiteFeather

Harlequin Desire

Sons of Country

Wrangling the Rich Rancher
Nashville Rebel
Nashville Secrets

Daughters of Country

Hot Nashville Nights

Visit her Author Profile page at Harlequin.com or www.sheriwhitefeather.com for more titles.

You can also find Sheri WhiteFeather on Facebook, along with other Harlequin Desire authors, at Facebook.com/harlequindesireauthors!

One

Alice

I parked at the end of Spencer Riggs's long, narrow driveway and glanced out at the vine-covered arbor leading to his porch. Along the path, potted plants grew in colorful disarray, giving me a sense of elegant chaos.

I was trying not to panic about this meeting, but Spencer was different from my other Nashville clients. He was a former lover of mine, a dark shadow from my past.

Was it any wonder I was nervous?

I stayed in my car for a few more minutes, still gazing out the windshield. The music industry adored Spencer, and so did the women in this town. According to the social media buzz, he was quite the catch. An award-winning songwriter with a reputation for being a creative genius. A handsome twenty-eight-year-old who lived in a beautifully renovated old house and rescued abused and abandoned dogs. Talk about a new life. He didn't even have a goldfish when I knew him. He'd been working as a bartender back then, struggling to sell his songs.

I'd heard rumors that he was considered unattainable now. Of course, that just made women want him all the more. But in spite of his female following, he kept his affairs private. No one was out there bragging about being with him. He wasn't dropping names, either.

I found that curious, considering my dirty-sex history with him. Our hookups only lasted a few months, but I'd never forgotten how wild he was in bed. Or how troubled he'd made me feel. During that time, I'd had all sorts of emotional problems, and my affair with him had only fueled the fire.

These days, I was a freelance fashion stylist, and I would be dressing him for an upcoming magazine photo shoot. The magazine was willing to provide Spencer with one of their stylists, but he wanted to hire me instead, footing the bill himself and paying me directly. I didn't relish the idea of working for him, but what could I do?

My career was still in its early stages, and I was in no position to turn down an A-lister. His name would look good on my resume. But even more importantly, a world-renowned photographer was booked for the shoot. If I impressed him, this could be a game changer for me. And the final kicker? I'd spent way too much money over the years, and the hefty sum I'd received from a legal settlement when I was just nineteen years old was dwindling. If I didn't take this job and use it to my best advantage, I might never get out of the hole I created.

I drew a breath, then exited my car and made my way to Spencer's door. It had rained heavily earlier, but it was just drizzling now.

I rang the bell, and he answered quickly enough.

Holy cow. It had been five years, and Spencer was hotter than ever. He stood tall and fit, with a naturally tanned complexion and straight, collar-length brown hair, parted on the side and swept across his forehead. His deep-set eyes were dark, almost black, and his jaw was peppered with beard stubble. He had strong features: prominent cheekbones and a wide, luscious mouth. He wore a plain beige T-shirt, threadbare jeans, torn at one knee, and leather sneakers. His left arm boasted a full-sleeve tattoo, but the ink was white, making it look like scarring against his dark skin.

"That's new," I said.

He blinked at me. "What?"

"The tattoo."

"Oh, yeah." He was staring at me as though he was having the same knee-jerk reaction that I was having to him. "How have you been, Alice?"

"Fine." When he shifted his stance, my long-lost libido clenched. I'd been celibate since I'd shared his bed, swearing off men until the right one came along—a decision that my reckless hookups with him had obviously factored into. I'd already been using sex to fill the void inside me and being passionately consumed with him had intensified the ache.

"Do you want to come in?" he asked.

I nodded, wondering what he would think if he knew how cautious I was now. Or how badly I wanted to fall in love, get married and have babies.

He stepped away from the door, and we both went inside.

He was no longer staring at me, but I suspected that he wanted to take another long, hard look. We'd had sex in every room of his old apartment. One of his favorite activities had been doing body shots off my navel or from in between my breasts. Everything we'd done together had been hard and fast, including midnight rides on his motorcycle.

He led me to the living room, where a shiny red piano made a bold statement. His house boasted vintage charm, but was rife with contemporary updates.

He wasn't born and bred in Nashville. He was originally from LA and never knew his father. He was raised by a single mother but somewhere along the way, she'd died and he'd moved in with an aunt and uncle. He'd only given me vague details. He knew far more about me than I did about him.

He gestured to an impressive wet bar and coffee station. "Can I get you anything?"

"That's all right. I'm okay." To keep my hands busy, I smoothed my top. I wore an oversize tunic, skinny jeans and thigh-high boots that served me in the rain. My bleached blond hair was short and choppy, left over from my cowpunk phase. It was the only wild side of myself that I'd held on to.

He sat across from me, illuminated by the cloudy light spilling in from the windows. My mind was whirring, working feverishly about how I was going to dress him. I envisioned a variety of looks, ranging from rebellious to refined. From what I recalled, he'd never really cared much about clothes, except when he was removing mine.

"You came highly recommended," he said, jarring me out of my thoughts. "Kirby suggested that I hire you."

I gaped at him. *"Kirby Talbot?"* The country superstar who'd destroyed my mother, who'd promised to buy her songs, but had merely slept with her instead. "Seriously, Spencer?" He knew damned well that I hated Kirby. Not only had Kirby ghosted my mother after their affair, he'd filed a restraining order against her when she'd tried to contact him again.

His heartless actions were a tragedy from which Mama had never recovered. I never got over it, either. Her depression had destroyed me when I was young. Now that I was grown up, Kirby kept trying to fix it. But I couldn't forget the pain he'd caused.

I frowned at my former lover. I was aware that he'd written some recent hits for Kirby, but beyond that I didn't know what their relationship entailed. "Just how chummy are you?"

"He's actually become a mentor to me." Spencer

twisted one of the threads that looped across the hole in his jeans, then looked up, his gaze instantly riveted to mine. "I couldn't have gotten sober without him."

I blinked, then glanced at the bar, where bottles of liquor were clearly visible. "You're a recovering alcoholic?"

He continued looking at me. "I've had a problem with it for years. Don't you remember how drunk I used to get?"

"Yes, but I didn't know it was an addiction. I just thought you liked to party." I was feeling foolishly naïve. All those slurred, sexy nights, all those body shots. "Why do you have a fully stocked bar now?"

"I keep it around for guests." He ran his gaze over me. "I can resist the temptation."

I hoped he resisted his drink of choice far better than he was resisting his renewed attraction to me. The air between us had gone unbearably thick. *Temptation*, I thought. So much temptation.

And on top of that, I wasn't convinced that if push came to shove, he wouldn't fall off the wagon. He still seemed restless to me. "How long have you been sober?"

"Two years, three months, five days and—" He removed his phone from his pocket and checked the time "—six hours." He glanced up and laughed a little. "Give or take."

His jokey remark didn't ease my concern. "I'm glad you're trying to turn your life around." I would at least give him credit for that. "But you know what sucks? That I used to tell you what a jerk Kirby was, but you still managed to bond with him. You'd never even met him when I was with you."

He scowled. "Well, I got to know him later. And what was I was supposed to do? Shun him because of you? He's been trying to make amends with you for years."

I tightened my spine, sitting ramrod straight. Spencer used to support my hatred of Kirby, but now he was siding with the enemy. "Did you hire me as a favor to Kirby? Is that what this is all about?"

"No." His scowl deepened.

"Then why did you hire me?"

He shrugged. "For old times' sake, I guess."

Meaning what, exactly? That he was curious to see me? That didn't make me feel any better. Our affair had started in the gutter. We'd hooked up on Tinder, strictly for the sex. I'd been all of twenty then. Young and promiscuous.

I gave him a pointed look. "You still shouldn't have blindsided me about Kirby."

He shook his head. "I don't understand your reluctance to forgive him. He apologized for what he did to your family, not just privately but in a press conference, too. He bought the rights to your mom's songs from you and your sister and made good on his promise to market them. You got a nice settlement from him."

"It wasn't enough to last forever. Going to college and starting a new business wasn't cheap." I'd definitely spent a huge chunk on those things. But I'd blown tons of it, too. Not that I was going to admit that to Spencer. But in my defense, I was still running wild when I first got the money.

"Yeah, well, it's just crazy that you won't give Kirby a chance." He shook his head again. "Your sister is even married to his oldest son."

"That doesn't mean I have to accept Kirby the way she has. Besides, Mary has a softer heart than I do." She was also blissfully happy with Brandon and their children. I was still waiting around for my dream man.

We sat quietly, until he said, "When Kirby first recommended you as my stylist, he didn't know that I was acquainted with you. He knows now, though. I told him that we used to date."

"Why in the hell did you do that?" I could have strangled Spencer, murdered him for real.

"Because it was too weird for me to pretend that we were strangers."

"And now he thinks that we went out, way back when?"

He stared me down. "Would you have preferred that I told him the truth?"

"Of course not." I didn't want Kirby knowing my personal business. "I would have preferred that you kept your trap shut."

"At least I made it sound respectable."

"Whatever." I didn't want to talk about it anymore.

"Well, you know what?" he snapped. "Maybe you and I shouldn't work together."

Screw him, I thought. "You're going to fire me already?"

He jerked his head. "I might."

"Whatever," I said again. I was too damned mad to care.

In the tense silence that followed, I studied the pale ink on Spencer's arm. His tattoo was a predominantly Native American design. Kirby had a half-Cherokee son named Matt with one of his former mistresses, and Spencer was of mixed origins, too. He'd never told me what tribe he was from, though. When I'd asked, he'd claimed it didn't matter. But now he was covered in artwork that seemed to prove otherwise.

I brazenly said, "It's interesting that Kirby has a son with a similar heritage to yours. If I didn't know better, I'd think that you could be one of his kids, too."

He rolled his eyes. "Yeah, right."

"Maybe you actually are his son," I taunted him. Not because I believed he was Kirby's heir, but just because I wanted to get back at him for not keeping quiet about us. "You might be his kid, and you don't even know it. With the way Kirby messed around, he could have dozens of illegitimate children out there."

He sighed. "Go ahead and make up whatever stories you want. But biologically, him being my father is impossible. Kirby is white, and so was my mom."

For some unknown reason, I'd always assumed that his mother had been Native American, but Spencer's brown skin had obviously come from the father he'd never met. I swallowed my pride and apologized. "I'm sorry. I shouldn't have said any of that." I had no right to bring his family into my foolishness. I made a sheepish expression and said, "Truce?"

He lifted his eyebrows, making me wait for his reply. Was he going to tell me to get lost? Had I blown this job? Had my stupidity gotten in the way?

"You're something else," he said a few heartbeats later. He didn't sound amused. But he didn't sound angry anymore, either. He expelled a breath and added, "But you always were feisty."

I used to be a full-on brat, but I wasn't going to cop to it now. I flashed a hopeful smile. "You're not firing me?"

"I guess not." He glanced at my lips, as if he was remembering the taste of them.

He stood and walked over to the bar. Seconds ticked by, or maybe it was minutes. I wanted to break the silence, but I couldn't think of an intelligent thing to say. I was remembering the taste of his lips, too.

"Are you sure I can't get you anything?" he asked.

I blinked at him. "Anything?"

"To drink. I'm going to have a ginger ale."

Actually, I was getting thirsty. Or maybe my mouth had gone dry as a reaction to him. The air between us had gone thick again. "I'll have what you're having."

"Do you want yours on ice?"

"Yes, please."

He turned, opened the mini fridge and poured my drink.

"Here you go." He came toward me with my ginger ale, and I reached out to take it.

He returned to the mini fridge, retrieved a soda for himself and took a swig directly from the can. I sipped my drink, the ice clinking in my glass. He leaned against the bar, facing me now. So tall, so dark, so damned handsome.

I steadied my voice and asked, "Is the photo shoot going to be here at your house?"

"Yes, it'll be here, showcasing how I live."

He kept drinking his ginger ale, with the off-limits bottles of hard liquor behind him. The wine rack on the bar was full, too. He was surrounded by the forbidden.

I was, too. Not the alcohol. That wasn't a problem for me. My forbidden was Spencer himself. Crazy as it was, I was about to invite myself to his bedroom.

"Do you mind if I look in your closet to get a feel for your wardrobe?" I asked.

"No, I don't mind." He gestured to his attire. "Expect lots of jeans. Fancy clothes aren't really my forte."

He waited until I stood, then headed for a set of etched-glass doors that led to another part of the house. As I followed him, he glanced back and said, "I like your boots, by the way. They're really…"

He didn't finish his statement. I suspected he was going to say "sexy" or "hot" or something of that nature. But he let it drift instead.

I let it go, too. He guided me down a hallway riddled with artfully framed movie posters. I spotted a black-and-white still from *The Wild One*, featuring a young and defiant Marlon Brando, and my interest was piqued. The actor sat on a Triumph motorcycle, sporting 1950s biker gear. I knew the history behind his clothes. I'd taken a class about fashion in film.

Spencer opened the door to the master suite. "This is it, where my closet is."

The first thing I saw was his king-size bed. It sat on a platform frame constructed from natural wood. The covers were tan and gold. Masculine. Overall, his room was warm and inviting, with an adjoining bathroom and French doors leading to the backyard. The curtains were open, with a view of his pool. Beyond it was acres of grass.

"Your home is beautiful," I said. "I should have told you that when I first got here." I wandered over to the doors and peered out.

He joined me, pointing to a flagstone path that cut through the grass. "My guesthouse is out that way. I turned it into a dog rescue. I have a slew of people who help me with it. Some are paid employees and some are volunteers."

"I don't have any pets." I wondered if that made me lacking. "Mary and Brandon have a husky named Cline. My niece and nephew adore him. He was Brandon's dog before he met my sister, and now Cline is the family dog."

"I have two dogs."

"You do? Where are they?"

He mock-whispered, "Hiding under the bed." He smiled and said in a normal tone, "They're just checking you out, deciding if you can be trusted. They were my first rescues, and I couldn't bear to let them go, so they became mine."

Curious about his companions, I glanced at the foot of the bed. Sure enough, there were two little white faces poking out from under it.

"They're adorable," I said. "They look like dust mops with eyeballs. What are they, actually?"

"Maltese. Normally they're a fearless breed, but Cookie and Candy came from a traumatic situation. Once they get used to you, you'll see whole new sides of them."

"How long will it take for them to get used to me?"

"I don't know. Sometimes they come around quickly and sometimes they don't. If they're agreeable on the day of the shoot, we might use them in some of the pictures. They already met the photographer and liked him."

"That's good." The shoot was a little over a month away, so there was plenty of time for his dogs to cozy up to me. "Has the photographer discussed his vision with you and what sort of image he wants you to project?"

Spencer winced a little. "He said they want to go with a reformed bad-boy thing."

I cocked my head. "You don't like that idea?"

"It's okay, I guess. We all have a brand these days, and that's how mine is unfolding."

"I can certainly build your style around it." I knew just how bad he used to be. "I should check out your clothes now."

"We can go into my closet together. It's big enough for both of us."

That was true. His walk-in was more like a room.

Still, once we were inside, I imagined turning out the light and pressing my mouth against his. The first time I'd ever kissed a boy was in a closet. But not the urgent way I used to kiss Spencer.

To keep myself sane, I inhaled the fabric-cluttered air. His clothes smelled clean and fresh. He was right. There were a lot of blue jeans.

"I have a few suits," he said, and showed me the garment bags.

As I unzipped them to check the labels, I almost felt as if I were undressing him. I shivered at the memory.

He stood back and his gaze roamed over me, and I hastily said, "You have great taste for someone who doesn't place much importance on fancy clothes." His Italian-cut suits were impeccably tailored. He'd certainly spent some money on them.

Spencer shrugged, but not in a casual way. He seemed as if he had a lot on his mind. I knew the feeling.

Finally, he said, "When I was a kid, my aunt and uncle used to make me dress up for their dinner parties and whatnot, so I guess some of it stuck. I know that I never told you this before, but they were rich as sin."

I widened my eyes. He'd been raised with wealth and privilege? I hadn't seen that coming. But as vague as he'd always been, how would I have known? "How old were you when you went to live with them?"

He frowned. "Ten. That's when my mom died."

I understood his pain, the ache I heard in his voice. I knew what being motherless was like. My poor mama had succumbed to heart failure when I was eighteen, and I missed her every day. I preferred to think of her before she got so depressed, but it wasn't easy. I was eleven when Kirby had damaged her, when her struggles had begun. For me, those memories ran deep, and so did my rebellious behavior. By the time I was in high school, boys were writing my name on bathroom walls.

"No child should have to lose a parent," I said.

Spencer stepped a little closer. "My mom was an aspiring actress, but she didn't live to see her dream fulfilled. Mostly she worked at department stores, walking around spritzing perfume." He paused to clear his throat. "My aunt and uncle are in commercial real estate, with properties all over the world. When my mother passed, they carted me off to their big, stiff mansion in Hidden Hills. It's a gated community in LA."

Were they as controlling as they were rich? Based on his description, I assumed that they were. I'd grown up in a low-income area in Oklahoma City, where Mama struggled to pay our bills. "They sound pretty uppity."

"I learned all sorts of proper things from them." He gestured to the suit in my hand. "I know at least twenty different ways to tie a tie."

"Well, I've got you beat." Had he rebelled because of them? Were they part of his cause and effect? "I've perfected thirty. Knots are one of my specialties. Ties, scarves. I can do it all."

"Too bad we never discussed this before." He teasingly added, "We could've had some bondage fun back in the day."

"That's not funny." But I laughed anyway, sensing that he needed to lighten the mood and quit talking about his family.

I closed the garment bags and continued looking through his things. He had a couple of high-quality motorcycle jackets. I reached for one of them and ran my hand along the leather.

Before I stroked it too much, I turned my attention to the bottom shelf, where his shoes were perched. I noticed a pair of wonderfully scuffed biker boots with a vintage vibe, similar to the ones Brando had worn in *The Wild One*.

"Is it safe to assume that you still ride?" I asked.

"Yeah, Harleys are still my thing."

I checked out more of his shoes. He had a nice selection of cowboy boots. "Horses, too?"

He nodded. "I have a barn just beyond the rescue with two really pretty palominos." He looked directly at me. "But you already know I'm partial to blondes."

I forced myself to breathe, with his all-too-hungry gaze practically devouring me.

We exited the closet, and I felt my skin flush. I was horribly warm, overheated, in fact.

After an awkward beat of silence, I headed for the French doors and said, "It's raining again." I wished I could open them, go outside and let the water drench every anxious inch of me.

He came over to where I was. "It's not supposed to let up until tomorrow."

We stood side by side, body heat mounting between us. Even the dogs under the bed had crept closer to the edge, waiting to see what we might do.

"So, what happens now?" he asked.

I assumed he meant in relation to me being his stylist. But my mind was spinning in all sorts of directions. "Once we work out a budget, I'll shop for you. Then I'll bring everything here for you to try on. We can incorporate some of your belongings into the designs, too." I wanted to see him in those motorcycle boots. I loved how battered they were.

"I'll also need to take your measurements before I leave here today. That'll give me an accurate handle on your sizes. I can't just rely on the labels from your clothes."

"That's fine." He shifted his feet, and one of the dogs pawed at his shoe.

He reached down to pick her up, and she cuddled in his arms. I didn't try to pet her. Touching her would bring me too close to him. I was already stressing about taking his measurements.

I'd promised myself that I wouldn't get intimately involved with anyone unless it promised to develop into a meaningful relationship. But now I was fantasizing about hooking up with my old lover and having hot and dangerous sex with him again. Did Spencer have the power to turn me back into the reckless girl I used to be?

God, I hoped not.

But a shameful part of me wanted to find out.

Two

Spencer

Damn, I thought. Alice McKenzie was doing a number on me all over again, just like the first time I'd met her. We'd both swiped right on Tinder, and after one flirtatious chat, I'd invited her to the trendy club where I used to work. Later that night, she'd followed me to my apartment, and I had the best sex of my life.

But things were different now.

So much different.

I hadn't even kissed anyone since I quit drinking. For now, I was abstinent.

Painfully abstinent.

Funny, but I hadn't actually thought of it as painful until today, and that was because of Alice. Pretty

Alice, with her sultry brown eyes, spiky blond hair and killer boots. As much as I hated to admit it, I'd never really gotten her out of my head. I'd thought about her a lot over the years. The abrupt way she'd ended our affair had always bothered me. At the time, we'd still been going hot and heavy, and she'd left me wondering what I'd done wrong. Even now, I was trying to figure out what Alice really thought of me. Was that the reason I'd hired her to work for me? Was I looking for some sort of closure?

While my thoughts scattered, Cookie whined to be free. I set her down, and she scampered back to Candy. The two of them stared up at Alice as if she was a spaceship that had just landed. I was probably looking at her that way, too. I used to call her Alice in Spencerland when she was in my bed. I didn't know what to call her now.

"Do they sleep here?" she asked.

My brain fogged. "I'm sorry. What?"

"The dogs. Do they sleep in your room?"

I shook my head. "They have their own beds in another room. But they like hanging out in here. They spend a lot time at the rescue, too, playing with the other dogs."

"That's nice that they have other company." She hesitated before she said, "I should probably take your measurements now."

I'd been measured by tailors before. When I was a kid, it seemed like a regular occurrence, given how fast I was growing and with all of the dress-up occasions I'd been forced to attend. But knowing that

Alice was going to put her hands on me was a whole other matter.

She reached into her bag and removed a tape measure. She got out an iPad, too. "I'm going to do your chest first. Don't flex or anything. Just stand normally."

I did as she asked, and she wrapped the tape measure under my armpits and around the fullest part of my chest. She recorded my size on her iPad.

She did my neck and sleeve length and recorded those sizes, too. When she got to my waist, my stomach muscles jumped. But she kept going. She put a finger between my body and the tape measure, giving me room to breathe. My inseam was next, a measurement that was going to require her get on her knees in front of me. She instructed me to remove my shoes, which I did.

When she dropped down and ran the tape measure from the lowest part of my crotch to my foot, I watched her, remembering the erotic things she used to do to me while she was on her knees.

I could've kicked myself for letting my mind go there. Were her thoughts straying in the same direction? I did my damnedest not to get aroused, and she seemed to be doing her damnedest to be quick and efficient.

She said, "I need to measure your feet, too."

"Sure. Okay." I couldn't protest, even if it meant that she had to stay on her knees.

She had one of those devices in her bag that they

used in shoe stores. She placed it in front of me, and I stepped onto it.

Afterward, she stood and fussed with her bag. I put my sneakers back on. There was awkward energy between us. She was the first woman I wanted since I got sober, and I wasn't sure how to deal with it. There was no denying that she was as attracted to me as I was to her. That much, I could feel. But feeling it and acting on it were two different things.

She said, "I should probably get going."

I searched my brain for an excuse to keep her. Regardless of the effect she was having on me, I didn't want her to leave. "Why don't you stick around and let me show you the rescue?"

She bit down on her bottom lip. "I am curious to see it."

I'd always been fascinated by the shape of her mouth. Her cranberry-colored lipstick intrigued me, too. It made her look dangerously kissable.

I broke my stare. "Let's grab our jackets and go."

She glanced out the glass doors, where the rain was pounding even harder now. "I left my hoodie in the car. I'll have to go back and—"

"I can loan you something." She'd already measured my body and handled some of my clothes. Her borrowing a jacket from me was the least of my concerns. I gestured to the closet. "You can choose what you want. Pick one out for me, too. Doesn't matter which one." I had plenty to go around.

"Okay." She returned to my closet.

Once again, my thoughts drifted to the past and the

things Alice and I used to do. We'd always had sex at my place. I don't know why she'd never invited me to hers. At the time, I hadn't bothered to ask. I hadn't been big on conversation then. But now it made me curious to see how she lived. Was she neat and tidy? Or did she keep things strewn about? I envisioned her being beautifully messy. I'd been taught to be orderly, even when I was torn up inside.

She came back with two basic hoodies, gray for her and black for me. We slipped them on. The one she was wearing was big on her. She was only five-four, five-five at the most, with a slim build. I was six-two with plenty of muscle. Somehow, though, our hip-thrusting always seemed to work, even when we were standing in the shower, getting soaking wet.

"Ready to see the rescue?" I asked. "It's about a five-minute walk." Just long enough for us to get wet, I thought.

She gazed out the French doors, assessing the weather. "Sure. Let's do it." She lifted her hood.

We ventured outside, and I led the way, past the pool and onto the flagstone path, with the rain beating down on us.

I glanced over at Alice and noticed how troubled she suddenly looked, her expression as dark as the clouds. Was she thinking about me? About us? Or did she have Kirby on her mind?

Her opinion of him disturbed me, especially with how much I'd come to care for him. I trusted him with my inner feelings, something I'd never done with anyone else before. He understood my tortured psyche. I could confide in him about anything. Yet I'd lied to him about Alice, pretending that she and I used to go on casual dates. Not that Kirby was naïve. He knew that I was a drunk back then and that Alice used to party. But I'd played down my relationship with her, making it seem light and easy. In spite of her hatred for him, he was fiercely protective of her, so I figured the truth wouldn't have sat well with him, anyway. Granted, what he'd done to Alice's mother was wrong. But he was sorry for the pain he'd caused and truly wanted to ease Alice's suffering. I admired him for that.

I said to her, "Kirby told me that you helped choose the artist who recorded your mother's songs. That Tracy Burton was your top pick."

She snuggled deeper into my jacket, tucking her hands into the pockets. "At the time, I wanted someone who was new to the business, but who understood the importance of Mama's music, too. Tracy and I have become really close since then. I guess you could say that she's my BFF now."

"Then it sounds like things worked out." I'd never met Tracy or worked with her, so I wasn't about to comment on how fleeting her fame had been. She'd had a great run with her debut and the songs Alice's mother had written, but as far as I knew, things had gone downhill from there.

I felt fortunate for my skyrocketing career. I'd come to Nashville with nothing, and now I was a Grammy Award-winning, highly sought-after songwriter. My aunt and uncle had refused to help me along the way, and I hadn't heard from them since. Not one measly phone call, congratulating me on my success.

Alice and I continued walking, with the rain still falling between us. The path narrowed, and I stepped onto the grass, giving her more room.

When we arrived at the rescue, we both wiped our feet and removed our damp jackets, hanging them on hooks in the entryway.

I introduced Alice to the staff and showed her around. The guesthouse had been remodeled to my specifications. We had kennels for when we needed them, but we also had canine-friendly rooms where the dogs could nap and play and socialize. There were tons of outdoor activities, too, on nicer days.

"This is a wonderful setup," Alice said, as we stood near the kitchen.

"We do our best." At the moment, a volunteer was preparing a meal for one of our newest residents, a poor little pup with a digestive disorder. "We have quite a few special-needs dogs."

"Are they difficult to place?"

"Yes." It was an unfortunate reality and one we faced daily. "Finding the right homes for them can be challenging."

Alice went quiet. The she asked, "What makes you do all of this, Spencer?"

I automatically replied, "I just want to make a difference in the world." That was my standard response, what I'd gotten used to saying. But it went deeper than that, so much deeper. I'd felt like a stray dog when I'd first landed on my aunt and uncle's doorstep. They'd fed me and clothed me and taught me to sit up and beg, rewarding me when I behaved and punishing me when I didn't. But I knew that no matter what I did, I would always be the mongrel they never really wanted.

During my darkest days, I used to fantasize about searching for my father, a man who didn't even know I existed. Sometimes I still thought about it.

"You have made a difference," Alice said.

For a second, I didn't know what she meant. Then I realized that she was referring to the rescue.

"Do you want to meet our mascot?" I asked. "He's a three-year-old English bulldog who runs the show around here. We're not going to adopt him out. He loves greeting people in the office, so that's where he is most of the time. He's Candy and Cookie's best buddy, too."

She smiled. "I'd love to meet him. What's his name?"

"We call him Peterbilt. Pete for short. We chose that name because he'll come at you like an eighteen-wheeler, pestering you to pet him."

An amused expression brightened up her face, making her even prettier than she already was. "I'm going to be delighted to make his acquaintance, I'm sure."

I took her to the office, a woodsy room that overlooked one of the fenced yards. For now, the office was vacant. No one was manning the desk. Pete lounged in his doggie bed, but when he caught sight of us, he roused himself quickly and ran toward us. He gave me a sloppy grin and made a beeline for Alice, barreling right into her.

She nearly tripped, and I grabbed her arm before she fell. She burst into a hearty laugh. Pete was a comical dude, with droopy eyes, a massive jaw and crooked teeth. Short and stout, with thick white wrinkles, he weighed about fifty pounds, moved with a crablike gait and drooled excessively.

Alice dropped to the floor to pet him, and he climbed onto her lap. I sat across from them and reached over to scratch his ears.

"Did you find yourself a new girlfriend there, buddy?" I asked him.

He grinned at me again. He was in canine heaven, but I could hardly blame him. I knew how it felt to be physically close to her. She wrapped her arms around him, soaking up his affection, and I envied him for charming her so easily. Of course, I'd done that, too, way back when.

"Can I bring him a toy next time I come by?" she asked. "Would that be okay?"

"Sure. You can bring him whatever you want." I wasn't going to deny Pete. Or her. She seemed to need to connect with him. "He's good about sharing his toys with the other dogs, too. He isn't territorial."

She lifted her eyebrows. "Not even with his girl-friends?"

"No, not even with them."

"I guess he has a lot of female companions, then."

"He has enough to keep him busy. But he's neu-

tered, so it's not the real deal. He still likes the ladies, though." Nonetheless, I didn't think it was the
dog's girlfriends who interested her. I suspected that
she was fishing to see who I slept with these days.
I furrowed my brow and asked, "Will you tell me
something?"

She squinted. "What?"

"Did I hurt you? In the past, I mean."

Her breath rushed out. "What makes you think
that?"

"Because you're the one who ended it, who just
texted me one day and said that you wouldn't be back.
I know we weren't committed to each other or anything, but it didn't seem like you were getting tired
of me, at least not when we were together. But I must
have done something to upset you."

She frowned. "It doesn't matter. It's over."

"Come on. Tell me what I did." I wasn't letting up,
not until I understood it better.

"Just drop it, Spencer."

"Tell me." I prodded her again.

"Fine." Her gaze slammed into mine. "I stopped
seeing you because I needed to be someone new. To
change my ways. To quit sleeping with men who
didn't care about me."

Her remark stung. But it was true. I hadn't cared
about myself then, let alone been capable of caring
for someone else. Now I was wondering if I should've
left well enough alone, instead of bugging her for a
response.

Then she said, "I probably shouldn't tell you this.

But I've actually done a good job of cleaning up my act. I've been celibate since I was with you."

Hell's fire. I merely stared at her. She hadn't had sex in five years? I couldn't have been more shocked.

After giving myself a second to comprehend her news, I said, "That's crazy, I mean, it's just so…" Before she misunderstood my reaction, I anxiously added, "I haven't been with anyone since I got sober."

Now it was her turn to stare at me. "I hadn't expected that you…" She shook her head. "It's weird that we both…"

Yeah, weird. I didn't even know what to say next.

She paused before she asked, "Do the women who follow you online know? Is that why they've been calling you unattainable?"

"No. They only say that about me because I haven't shown any interest in them." It wasn't because they knew that I gave up sex. "I prefer not to advertise what I do. Or don't do," I clarified.

She shifted the dog in her lap. He was falling asleep, his eyes drifting closed. "Me, neither."

It made me feel strange that I was the last guy she'd been with. The last man to be inside her. To make her come. It almost seemed romantic. But I knew that it wasn't.

"I really was the wrong guy for you," I said.

She sighed. "You were wrong for everybody back then."

"I still am." I shrugged off my discomfort. I wouldn't know how to do a relationship if it smacked me over the head. "Just call me Mr. Wrong."

"Well, that's funny," she replied solemnly. "Because after I ended it with you, I decided that I was going to wait for Mr. Right. That I wouldn't sleep with anyone until he came along. I'm hoping he'll be the man that I marry someday."

"The white picket fence thing." I'd never pictured her in that role. But I'd never pictured her anywhere, except naked in my bed.

She lobbed a curious look at me. "While we're on the subject, why did you stop having sex?"

Lucky for me, I had a solid answer. "Abstinence is part of my sobriety program."

"Through what? AA?"

"No, but it's something similar at a private rehab center. Kirby introduced me to it. We both attend meetings there." I explained without going into too much detail. "It's an outpatient program. Not one of those places where you check yourself in."

"And they advocate abstinence for two whole years? That seems like a long time for a program like that."

"Typically, it's no dating and no sex for a year. But after my first year was up, I just wasn't ready to jump back in."

She sent me another curious look, snaring me with her next question. "When will you be ready?"

"I don't have a guideline to follow." As badly as I wanted her, I was already losing ground. "I guess I'll just know. But for now, I'm still trying to figure myself out. What about you? Have you at least been on some dates?"

"Yes, but it never amounts to anything." Her shoulders drooped. "The chemistry just hasn't been there."

My chemistry with her was a bitch. I could feel it tightening its noose around me. "I haven't even kissed anyone."

She squeezed her eyes shut. "Me, neither."

I cleared my throat. "Not even on any of those dates?"

She opened her eyes. "I don't kiss on first dates anymore, and none of them ever got past that point." She glanced at the sleeping bulldog. "I'll bet Pete would kiss me if he could."

I watched her with anticipation. "Sloppy dog kisses don't count." But my mouth on hers would. I wanted to do it in the worst way.

When Alice lifted her head, our gazes locked. The rain was slashing against the office windows, intensifying the moment. Neither of us spoke, not one word, not one syllable.

I finally said, "I feel like I'm in junior high again."

She blinked at me. "Is that when you had your first kiss?"

"With tongues, yeah. How about you?"

She winced. "I was in elementary school. Fifth grade, at someone's birthday party. I went into a closet with a boy I liked."

"Damn, girl. You really were a wilding." I tried for a bit of humor. "Do you want to go back into my closet with me?"

She broke down and laughed. "You wish."

Darned right, I did. My heart jumped when I said,

"I can only imagine how good a kiss would feel after all this time."

"Really good," she said, her voice turning soft.

We stared longingly at each other. But we didn't lean forward or put our mouths together. It seemed too risky, too wrong. We were former lovers, in the midst of celibacy, and this wasn't a path either of us was supposed to be taking.

No matter how hot and satisfying it would be.

Three

Alice

I wanted to kiss Spencer, so help me I did. He was arousing me from the inside out, just the way he used to.

He ran a hand through his hair, and I went warm all over. I imagined running my hands through it, too. It fell across his forehead, the thick dark strands messy from the rain. God, he was tempting: so familiar, so gorgeous.

So celibate.

Somehow that should have made him seem safer, but it didn't. He was making me feel like a sex-starved mess. Spencer had changed, but he wasn't any better for me now than he was before. I needed someone who was ready to settle down and raise a family. I needed security, not a recovering alcoholic, trying to find himself.

To keep myself from staring at him any more than I already had, I glanced down at the dog. Pete was still out like a light.

"At least he isn't snoring," I said, trying to make regular conversation. We couldn't keep talking about how good a kiss would feel or how long it had been since we'd had sex.

Spencer seemed relieved that I changed the topic. He quickly replied, "Pete used to snore. He had breathing problems when we took him in. We had his palate surgically corrected. He had a few other health issues that we dealt with, too. As you can see, he's totally fine now."

"Where did he come from? What's his background?"

"He was left at a kill shelter, and his time was almost up when we heard about him." Spencer blew out a tight breath. "I guess his owner didn't think he was worth it. It makes me sick, the way some people treat their pets, as if they're just so damned disposable."

"I think the work you're doing here is wonderful." I was impressed by how nurturing he seemed and how much he obviously cared. Would he be a gentle lover now? There'd never been any sweetness during our affair, no snuggly warmth. As much as I'd wanted him to hold me afterward, he just hadn't been the type.

I shook away the memory. But somehow, the longing remained. "What about Candy and Cookie? Were they left at a shelter, too?"

"They were orphaned. They'd been alone in the house with their owner when she accidentally fell down the stairs. She died on impact, from a spinal cord injury." He frowned and continued with, "The dogs were so traumatized, they dug their way out of the yard and started living on the streets. People tried to catch them, but they just kept running away. Then I found them hiding under my front porch."

"Really? You found them yourself?"

He nodded. "They were dirty and matted and covered in burrs. Candy's legs were scraped up, and one of Cookie's ears was torn. I called a mobile vet, and he came out to the house and tended to them. Since there wasn't anyone associated with their owner who was able to take them, I offered to let them stay with me until I found another home for them." He drew his knees up. "But I got attached and kept them instead. After that, I decided to start a rescue. There's a lot of work that's involved in running a place like this. It didn't happen overnight."

I pondered the story he'd told me. It was certainly better than mulling over our past. "I never really thought about what happens to pets when their owners die."

"My mother died in a similar way. From a fall."

"Oh, my goodness. I'm so sorry." He'd mentioned his mom earlier, and now he was talking about the manner in which she'd left this earth. It didn't get more painful than that. I shuddered and asked, "Were you with her when it happened?"

"No." He glanced at his shoes, at the bits of mud and grass on them. "I was at school, and she was home, painting the beams in our apartment. The ladder tipped over, and she suffered a head injury." He kept studying his shoes. "She thought she was okay at first, but then she started feeling dizzy and confused and called a friend to take her to urgent care. But by then, her brain was already starting to swell."

He finally lifted his gaze. He'd done more talking today than he had in the entire time I'd known him.

Before he slipped back into his old silent ways, I said, "It must have been awful for you, going to live with your aunt and uncle after something so traumatic."

"Yeah. It pretty much sucked."

"Which one of them is your blood relative?"

"My aunt. She's my mother's older sister. They came from a dysfunctional family." He paused slightly. "Their dad was an alcoholic."

I gauged the discomfort in his eyes. Those dark, brooding eyes. "I heard it can be hereditary. The alcoholism," I added, making my meaning clear.

He shrugged it off. "My grandfather was a mean old cuss who died from liver disease. I hardly remember him."

"At least you weren't a mean drunk."

He snared my gaze. "I was rough with you in bed."

Was it necessary for him to remind me of that? "We were both rough with each other." I used to rake my nails all over him, clawing and scratching. "It's just what we did."

"I know, but I should have been gentler."

"It doesn't matter," I said, even if it did. I'd always left his apartment feeling lonely and confused.

He replied, "I'm sorry if I wasn't more romantic with you."

His apology went straight to my heart, making it skitter. "Is this part of your sobriety? Saying sorry to all of the women you never cuddled?"

No." He spoke lower, raspier. "I'm only saying it to you."

I tried to act normal, to not let my emotions show. "I appreciate your concern, but it isn't necessary."

He watched me, a bit too closely. "I just don't want you feeling bad about the past."

Or letting it affect the present? It was too late for that. I wasn't just struggling with my memories, I was troubled by his current association with Kirby, too.

"How well do you know my sister and Brandon?" I asked. I'd never told Mary about my affair with Spencer, and she'd never mentioned his name to me, either. But that didn't mean they weren't acquainted.

"I've never met Mary. Or Brandon. My friendship with Kirby doesn't extend to his kids. Not that I have anything against them. It's just easier for me to keep my relationship with him private."

"That makes sense, I suppose." It was easier for me, too, to keep my sister out of the loop. She knew that I used to sleep around and that I was waiting for the right man now. But we didn't have major conversations about it. Mary had been through enough with me when I was a kid, always worrying about my wild side. Before those reckless feelings came flooding back, I said, "I better get going."

Spencer frowned. "You don't have to run off."

"I'm not." Thankfully, I had a reason for leaving. "I'm having lunch with Tracy today, and it's all the way across town." I had plenty of time, but it was still a good excuse. Besides, I was eager to see her. Unlike Mary, I used Tracy as my confidante. I'd already told her about Spencer, talking about him on and off throughout the years, and now I would be telling her even more. "It was nice seeing the rescue and meeting Pete, but I really have to go."

He was still frowning. "Then I'll walk you to your car."

"All right. But how do I…?" I was concerned about startling the sleeping bulldog.

He bent over to help me. "Just roll him off you. He probably won't even wake up."

We moved Pete together, and he landed belly side up, with his feet in the air and his tongue lolling to one side.

"Told ya," Spencer said, and we both smiled.

I climbed up off the floor. He stood, too. At least the tension was gone. But I knew how quickly it could return.

We retrieved the jackets we'd worn, put them back on and left the rescue, heading back into the rain. We didn't chat along the way. But we'd said plenty already.

He took me through a side gate that led to his driveway, where I was parked.

I started to unzip his hoodie to return it to him, but he said, "You can keep it until next time."

"I have my own in the car."

"If you take it off now, you'll get soaked."

That was true. The rain was coming down hard. If only it would knock some sense into me. I was losing my mind, fantasizing about giving up my celibacy for him. Would he stop being abstinent for me, too?

Struggling to keep my wits about me, I deactivated the alarm on my Prius. Spencer looked as if he wanted to eat me alive. Or at least nibble me to death.

I imagined feasting on him, using my mouth in ways I knew he would enjoy. I glanced away, trying to keep my cool. Working for him wasn't going to be easy, but I couldn't bail out, not with how badly I needed this job.

"I'll be in touch," I said, forcing a professional air.

He nodded, and I ducked into my car and started the engine. He stood in the rain, looking tall and dark and shadowy. I put the shifter in reverse and backed out of his driveway.

Desperate to escape.

I wore Spencer's jacket to lunch. I could have switched to mine, but I was already wearing his. Or that's the excuse I used. Truth was, I just wanted to keep something of his next to me. My hunger for him was crushing my common sense.

I sat in the cramped entrance of the mom-and-pop diner and waited for Tracy to arrive. She wasn't late; I was actually a little early. But it gave me time to catch my breath. Or try to. There wasn't a table available yet, anyway.

When Tracy showed up, she breezed in like the rough-and-tumble country girl that she was. She'd been raised on a dusty old horse farm by her rodeo cowboy dad. Her mom died when she was in middle school. All these lost mamas, I thought. Hers, mine, Spencer's.

I stood to greet her, and we hugged. After we separated, I stood back and said, "Wow. Check you out."

Beneath her straw Stetson, her long brown hair tumbled over her shoulders, as pretty as could be. Her jeans fit her to a T, but she had one of those sensually curvy bodies that filled out every seam. Without makeup, she had wholesome features. But she knew how to doll herself up. Today, her eyes were as smoky as mine, only they were blue, like the sky on a brighter day.

"I'm trying to fool people into thinking I'm still a celebrity," she replied.

"You'll always be a star to me." She certainly looked the part, even if her success had been short-lived. She'd spent most of the money she'd earned fixing up her dad's property. She'd bought herself a place, too. But everything had faltered so quickly, she was fighting to keep her mortgage afloat. She'd been through hard times before. One of the things we had in common was growing up poor.

The hostess escorted us to a vinyl booth near a

window. When it came time to order, we both chose the special: baked macaroni and cheese and collard greens. Comfort food was another thing we had in common. So was sweet tea with lots of ice.

After they brought our tea, Tracy asked me, "How did your meeting with Spencer go?"

"Terrible." I didn't hold back. I was used to sharing my screwed-up feelings with her. "It was like going back in time, with how badly I want him again."

She reached for her glass. "Maybe you're just getting cabin fever. Or celibate fever, or whatever."

"He's celibate, too."

She gaped at me. "No way."

"Yes, way." He was as inactive as I was.

"Dang, really? A guy like him? Why is he keeping all that manliness to himself?"

I repeated what he told me, about him being a recovering alcoholic and abstinence being part of his program, even if he'd carried it out for longer than the usual year.

"Is he struggling with his sobriety?" she asked.

"He said that he can handle the temptation of drinking, but I think it's more difficult for him than he's willing to admit. Of course, that's just my opinion. I'm not an authority on addiction." Not unless my attraction to him fell into that category.

"It's tough to know what another person is going through. But we've all got some sort of problems, don't we?"

"Yes, we do." And mine were escalating now that I'd seen Spencer again. "You know what makes it harder? Spencer is super close to Kirby. Kirby even helped him with his sobriety."

"Yikes." Tracy screwed up her face. "That's major. You can't mess with that kind of bond."

"Don't I know it." Kirby had been clean and sober for a long time. But when he was drinking and using, he'd hurt a lot of people. He'd even published a best-selling biography about his wrongdoings. He'd left Mama out of the book, though. He didn't acknowledge her until after she died, for all the good that had done. "I hate how Kirby expects to be absolved for all of the terrible things he did."

She took a long, cool sip of her tea. "You're the only person out there who hasn't forgiven him."

And rightly so, I thought. "Speaking of apologies… Spencer said he was sorry for not being more romantic when we were together."

She watched me with empathy in her eyes. "I'll bet that made seeing him even harder for you."

"I'm just glad I have you to talk to." Without her, I'd really be lost.

Our conversation halted when the waitress appeared with our specials. After she left, we dug into our meals.

A few minutes later, Tracy looked up from her plate and asked, "Did Spencer happen to mention that he's going to be working with Dash on his next album?"

"No, he didn't say anything about that." Dash Smith was Tracy's former fiancé. They'd gotten engaged years ago, when both of them were still trying to make it. But nowadays, Tracy was struggling again, and Dash was a big star. At the moment, he was off on a world tour. "How do you know Spencer is going to be working with Dash?"

"I read about it."

"You need to stop reading about Dash and following his career."

"I know." Beneath the brim of her hat, her expression turned tortured. "I'm a glutton for punishment."

I was, too, apparently, judging how badly Spencer was affecting me. But my hang-up was based on lust. Somewhere in the pit of her broken heart, Tracy was still in love with her ex. "It's not healthy for you to obsess about him."

"I only do that because he's so famous now." She glanced toward the rainy window, then back at me. "I don't begrudge him his success. I know how hard he worked for it. Dash was poorer than you and I ever were. He barely had food on the table when he was growing up. But it's just so painful to see him out there, living the high life, while I can't even get another record deal." She blew out a sigh. "Even my indie career sucks."

"I hate that you're going through this." These days, Tracy was putting her music out there herself, without a label to back her. But nothing was really happening. She was barely getting any downloads, even though her songs were really good. "Just don't lose hope. You know how things can turn around in this business."

"They certainly turned around for Dash. He has

the number one country album in the world. He's even crossing over into the pop charts."

"I'll bet he's lonely on the road." Or I hoped that he was, for her sake.

She rolled her eyes. "Oh, sure. With all those groupies out there, he's probably suffering something awful."

"Maybe you should reconsider his offer to help you." She'd told me before that Dash had been reaching out to her. He'd even suggested them doing a duet.

"Are you kidding? I don't need his charity. When I top the charts again, it'll be because I earned it, not because I'm riding my ex's coattails."

"As much as I admire your principles, maybe you're being stubborn about this, Trace."

"Oh, yeah?" She shot me a silly grin. "At least I've gotten laid in the past five years."

"Okay, smart-ass." I laughed in spite of myself. "Punish me for being a good girl now."

She leaned forward, pressing against the table. "Do you think Spencer wants you as badly as you want him?"

"Yes, I do." I wasn't going to pretend otherwise. I'd seen it on his face; I'd felt it from his reactions to me.

She sat back in her seat. "I understand that you're waiting for the right guy, and I want nothing more than for you to find him and live happily ever after. But if something does happen between you and Spencer, it won't be the end of the world, will it? I mean, at least it'll be with someone who's being cautious about his sex life, too."

I swallowed the last of my mac and cheese. "That's your answer to my problems?"

"No, of course not." She gentled her voice. "But it seems pretty obvious that your attraction to him isn't going to go away anytime soon."

"Maybe not. But just thinking about being with him scares me." The man who'd triggered my celibacy, who'd made me long for a husband and children and everything else I was missing.

She gestured to our near-empty plates. "Do you want to share a piece of pie since we're almost done eating?" She pushed the free-standing dessert menu toward me. "It might make you feel better."

I could definitely use something sweet today. "Maybe I should get my own slice instead of us sharing."

I flipped through the laminated pages, even if my hunger for Spencer wasn't something a warm gooey pie was going to satisfy. But it was safer than Tracy's other suggestion.

I knew better than to slip back into bed with my old lover. I just needed to stay focused on working for him.

And nothing else.

Four

Spencer

I got up early, gulped down a ridiculously strong cup of black coffee and took a long, hot, stare-at-the-walls shower. After that, I spent the next few hours working on some new songs. Or trying to, anyway. I was distracted with thoughts of Alice.

When I'd first hooked up with her, I'd sympathized with her position that Kirby was a rich, spoiled, womanizing superstar who only cared about himself. But when I met him a few years later, I saw a strong and stable man sorry for his sins. He'd hurt lots of people. By no means was he perfect. Sometimes he could still be brash and arrogant. But overall, he had a damned fine heart.

I wasn't going to let Alice taint my opinion of him. But that wasn't my only problem with her. I wanted to strip her bare, all over again. I wanted to hold her in my arms afterward, too, and remove some of the stigma of what we'd done before.

Was that a foolish fantasy on my part? Me, trying to play the gentleman? In all honestly, I had no idea what kind of lover I would be now. What if I sucked at being romantic? Drunk or sober, what if that wasn't who I was?

Dragging Alice back into my mess wouldn't be fair. Beautiful, temperamental Alice, searching for Mr. Right. We didn't belong together, and I had no business wanting her.

I glanced at the bar, with its shiny glass bottles lined up in pretty rows. If I sat here long enough, steeped in a woman from my past, would I get the familiar urge to drink?

Fighting my fears, I rose from my piano seat and moved about the room, telling myself that I could handle any hardship that came my way. But because she had me tied up in knots, I decided this would be a good day for a meeting. I knew the next one was at two o'clock. I had the schedule memorized.

I texted Kirby, asking if he would be there. We were part of a group that included a number of celebrities. In this town, it was mostly music industry folk. Our counselor was a heavily tattooed dude named Sam who'd seen and done it all. There was nothing you could say that would surprise Sam.

My phone signaled a text. It was Kirby, telling me

that he planned to go. I replied, letting him know that I would see him at the clinic.

I wasn't going to discuss my attraction to Alice with the group. I couldn't tell my story without revealing the edgy stuff I used to do with her, and I couldn't do that in front of Kirby, not without putting my sordid history with her on display. It was better left unsaid, not just for Kirby's peace of mind, but for mine and Alice's, too.

The meeting brought a bit of calm to my storm, and once it ended, Kirby invited me to his house. He lived in a plantation-style mansion, with a big sweeping staircase in the entryway and a sparkling stream running through the backyard. The property also included a recording studio and a menagerie of luxurious guesthouses. The entire compound had become known as "Kirbyville."

We shared a picnic bench near the stream, eating barbecued beef sandwiches and crispy fries his chef had prepared. The weather was nice, but already I was missing the rain.

I glanced across the table at Kirby. At sixty-six, he was a rough-looking guy, handsome in a country outlaw way, with hard lines in his face, graying hair and a salt-and-pepper beard. As a self-taught musician who'd worked his way up the ranks, he'd been around Nashville a long time. He had three sons, six grandkids, one supermodel ex-wife and countless everyday women who'd become his former mistresses.

What I'd told Alice was true: I'd never met anyone from Kirby's family. He kept trying to make it happen, though. He invited me to all of their gatherings—birthdays, holidays, the whole bit—hoping I'd warm up to the idea. But I always declined. After my mom died and my aunt and uncle took over, I'd lost my zest for being part of a family. Just being in those types of settings gave me a cold sweat.

"Did you ever contact Alice about that magazine thing?" Kirby asked, interrupting my thoughts.

"Yep. I sure did." I tossed out an easy vibe. The last thing I wanted was for him to notice how she affected me. "She came by my place yesterday. We'll be working together on the shoot."

"That's great. She's a little spitfire, isn't she? But I guess you already know that since you used to date." He paused. "How long did that last, anyway? You never really said much about it, other than how casual it was."

"I can't remember how long it was. A few months, maybe, here and there." In reality, it was every time we needed each other, day or night, which was pretty damned often. "Mostly we just hung out at clubs." At least that part wasn't a complete lie. On the night we'd arranged to meet, she'd sidled up to the bar where I'd worked, eager to check me out. She'd even dared me to spike her mojito mocktail with an illegal shot of rum. Serving alcohol to a hot little twenty-year-old could have cost me my job, but I was so taken with her, I almost did it. Later, when we were in the shower, having our second round of sex, I played a stupid game and poured Bacardi all over both of us.

Kirby dipped a fry in the glob of ketchup on his plate. "Did she tell you what a jerk she thinks I am?"

"Yes, but she told me that when I knew her before. She's always been testy about you."

"She talked to you about me before you and I ever met?" His voice turned tight. "Why are you just telling me this now?"

"Because it didn't seem relevant until now." I braced myself, waiting to see if he would accept my response without further scolding. Sometimes Kirby had the same fiery temper as Alice.

"You're right." He backed down. "It doesn't matter what she used to say about me. It's what she's still saying that counts. I love that I'm so close with her sister. Mary has completely forgiven me. But Alice..."

"She made a crack about you maybe being my dad. She didn't mean it, though. She was just messing with me."

"That's an odd thing for her to come up with." He gave his head a quick shake. "What made her say it?"

"Because of my heritage and your affair with Matt's mom. I hadn't really told her much about family before. She didn't know that my mom was white."

He met my gaze. "I'd be proud if you were my son. You're a good man, Spencer."

"Thank you." His words warmed my heart. "I'd be proud to have you as my dad, too." Unlike my aunt and uncle, he cared about my well-being.

He studied me, gently, kindly. "Are you still thinking of searching for your dad? You haven't mentioned him in a while."

"Yes, I still think about it." Only I had other things on my mind now that I'd seen Alice again. "But there's no rush."

"You definitely need to be ready to tackle something like that. But I think paternity matters. I'm still ashamed of what an awful parent I was to my boys when they were growing up."

"You've made up for that now." He'd done everything in his power to redeem himself. He loved his sons with every fiber of his being. He adored his grandchildren, too. His family was everything to him. "You're not the same guy you used to be."

"I wish Alice saw me the way you do."

"I wish she did, too. But with all of the pain it's causing both of you, maybe you should let it be for a while."

"And quit trying to win her affection? I can't do that. I need to keep trying."

I understood that he felt guilty about hurting her mom, but now I was worried that he might be taking it too far. With a bit of goofy sarcasm, I said, "Be careful, or someone might mistake you for being her dad."

I expected him to scoff at my remark, but that wasn't what happened. Instead, he flinched like I'd never seen him flinch before, squeezing the sandwich in his hand so hard some of the filling came out.

He replied, "You don't actually think…"

"Come on, Kirby, I was kidding. You being her dad is as impossible as you being mine." But seeing how panicked he was, my stomach dropped, like an elevator speeding to a bottom floor. "Isn't it?"

"Yes, of course." He eased his grip on his sandwich, even if he'd already done considerable damage to it. "Alice was eleven years old when I got involved with her mom."

I watched him stuff the mangled roll into his mouth and take a big messy bite.

"You didn't know her mom before then?"

He shook his head. He was still chewing his food.

"For real?" I pressed him. "Alice isn't your daughter?"

"No." He shifted in his seat. "Her old man was a truck driver named Joel McKenzie."

I remembered Alice telling me that her father had died when she was a baby. But that was all she'd ever said about him. "Did you have some sort of connection to Joel? Something Alice doesn't know about?" Was there more to this than Kirby was letting on?

He sent me an annoyed look. "I never even met the man." He put his sandwich down and pushed his plate away. "There's nothing nefarious going on. You're barking up the wrong tree."

"Then why are you acting so strange?"

"Because your joke about me being Alice's dad wasn't funny. You shouldn't have said something like that."

"You're right. I'm sorry." He'd never lied to me before, so why would he start now? In spite of his sullied past, I trusted him more than anyone. But here I was, lying to him about my affair with Alice. Should I admit that my relationship with her was more difficult than I'd let on? Or should I continue to keep it private? I chose the latter. This wasn't the time to open Pandora's box. "You deserve better than that from me, and so does Alice." I tried for a smile, hiding my feelings. "But we should probably change the subject now."

I didn't want to keep talking about Alice. Or thinking about her. Or wanting her. I was already anxious about seeing her again.

Two days later, Alice was back at my house with some clothes for me to try on. As she draped the garment bag over the back of my sofa, I caught sight of her profile. Her makeup was especially dramatic this afternoon. She'd even drawn those little lines in the corners of her eyes, for a catlike effect. It seemed fitting, considering what a hellcat she used to be in bed.

Would she still scratch and claw? Or would she be tamer now? I still had the foolhardy fantasy of being romantic with her. But I had feral urges, too, with how hot my blood ran every time she got near me. Not that it mattered. I wasn't planning on starting another affair. The issue wasn't how gentle or rough the sex would be. It wasn't her celibacy or my abstinence, either. Our problem was another man. The guy Alice had been waiting for. The Mr. Right who wasn't me.

"I brought a toy for Pete," she said.

I redirected my attention. I'd been too busy analyzing the affair we weren't going to have to notice the shopping bag at her feet. She reached into it and removed a squeaky toy shaped like a truck.

I let down my guard and smiled. It was damned cute. "He's going to love it."

She delved into the bag again. "I brought these for Candy and Cookie." Two more squeaky toys. "The cupcake is for Candy, because it has candy sprinkles on it. And the cookie is obviously for Cookie." She waved it around. "It looks like it already has a bite taken out of it."

Kill me now, but I wanted to take a lusty bite out of her. Being Mr. Wrong wasn't making my libido behave.

I shifted my stance and said, "Thank you for thinking of them. That was sweet of you."

"I hope the noise doesn't drive you crazy." She squeezed the cookie. "They're pretty loud."

"No worries. I'm used to it. They have lots of those types of toys. Sometimes I accidentally step on them. They always seem to leave them in my path."

"Then I better put these out of the way." She placed them on the coffee table. "Do you want to check out the stuff I brought for you?"

"Sure." As long we were on the subject of clothes, I took an appreciative gander at her outfit. She wore a flouncy little mini dress and ankle boots. Her legs were sleek and bare. Touchable, I thought. Or untouchable, depending how I looked at it.

She reached for the garment bag. "I still have a lot more shopping to do for you. But I wanted you to try on these shirts for now."

I would try on whatever she gave me. I'd hired

her to be my stylist. That was the point of her being here, even if it had become an exercise in restraint.

She continued talking. "I have this idea to put you in a formal shirt, hanging loose over a pair of holey jeans, like the ones you had on the last time I was here. We can even use those, if you want, rather than me getting you a new pair and tearing them up." She ran her gaze along the length of me. "You wear your jeans well."

I sported a different pair today that were less trashed. But the way she was looking at me was giving me goose bumps. Should I give up the fight and seduce her? For all I knew, she was already seducing me. My mind was too boggled to know who was doing what.

She unzipped the garment bag. "I got you three different shirts: a white, a black and a red one." She handed me the white shirt. "Let's try this first. Oh, and do you mind putting on your holey jeans, too?"

"No problem. What sort of shoes am I supposed to wear with this look?"

"I'm going to get you some leather oxfords. Dress shoes with a dress shirt. But I also want to try your biker boots and one of your motorcycle jackets with it, too. We'll just mix everything up and see what we get."

I went into my room to get dressed. I didn't invite her to come with me, but I wanted to. If this kept up, I was going to need a cold shower. Damn Alice, anyway.

I returned wearing the outfit she'd designed, down

to the boots and jacket. I left the shirttails loose, as she'd suggested. Her eyes lit up when she saw me.

"Oh, my God," she said. "That's so badass. Now let me see it without the jacket."

I ditched it and tossed it aside.

"We could do it both ways. You look rebellious, but handsomely refined, too."

Like the reformed bad boy that I was supposed to be? She admired me from every angle. I wanted to tell her to knock it off.

She handed me the black shirt. "Try this."

Instead of going back to my room, I changed where I was, and she watched as I bared my chest. She even bit down on her bottom lip. A nervous habit of hers. Well, it served her right, torturing me the way she was.

While I buttoned the black shirt, she came forward to help. "You missed some," she said.

She finished closing the rest of the buttons, and I inhaled her soft, floral scent. It wasn't the same fragrance that she used to wear, but it was just as enticing. I wanted her so badly, I imagined kissing her right here and now.

As she stepped back, her breath rushed out. "I like it, but the white was better, I think."

"Should I try the red now?" I was doing my best to concentrate on anything except sweeping her into my arms.

She nodded, and I switched shirts. This time she didn't help me button it. She seemed to recognize her mistake.

"That's definitely a possibility," she said, wringing her hands and twisting her fingers together.

Was she doing that to stop herself from touching me? My body was on fire, the embers burning hot and slow.

After a moment of heart-thundering silence, she said, "I think we should consider using a tie to create some contradiction."

"Torn jeans and a tie." I tried to sound as if I was mulling it over it. But mostly I was just battling the heat.

"I'll bring a selection with me next time. Or I'll go through yours and see if any of them will work. Your hair should be a little more tousled, too."

I tunneled my hands through it, pushing it away from my face. "Like this?"

"Yes, just like that." She breathed heavily again. "Also, will you roll up your shirtsleeves so part of your tattoo is visible?"

I followed her instructions. "Is this good?"

"It's perfect." She just stared at me.

I stared back at her, too, awkward as could be.

Then she said, "It's such a big tattoo. You must have put a lot of time and thought into getting that."

I broke eye contact and responded, "It was my gift to myself after I got sober." Getting inked was part of my growth, of my reawakening, of trying to create a new identity. But now it just felt like another facet of my uncertainty, of struggling to know who I was inside. Being around Alice wasn't helping those feelings, either, not with how hungry I was for her.

"I wanted something that seemed primal, that connected me to my heritage."

"You used to say it didn't matter. You wouldn't even tell me what tribe you were from."

"That's because I don't know what my tribal affiliation is. My mom met my dad in Arizona when she was on a road trip with some friends. I don't know if that's where he was from or if he was just passing through, too."

Alice leaned against the side of the sofa. "Was it a one-night stand?"

"That's what I gathered, yeah. I was pretty young when she first told me about him, so I pieced most of it together later. His name was Edward. No last name. I guess they never got around to sharing specifics. If she'd known that she was going to get pregnant by him, then maybe she would've taken notes."

"I wish you would have told me all of this before. You were always such a mystery."

I shrugged. Sometimes I still was, even to myself. My sobriety hadn't changed that. But at least I had my work to express myself. "Creative people are supposed to be mysterious."

She picked up the toy she'd gotten for Pete and glanced at it. "Did I ever tell you that my dad was a trucker?"

"No, but Kirby did. He also said that your dad's name was Joel."

She scowled. "Well, that figures, doesn't it? Kirby yapping to you about my personal business."

"He didn't say all that much. Just your dad's name

and profession." I wasn't about to admit that I'd accused Kirby of being her father. I wasn't in the mood to get my head chewed off. I'd already caught enough hell from him.

Her frown waned, making me relax a little. But I was still sort of jittery, too, always trapped in the middle with her.

She expelled a sigh. "Here's a tidbit that Kirby might not know about me, unless Mary told him. My parents named me Alice because my dad's favorite band was Alice in Chains. He wasn't into country, not like Mama. He preferred glam and grunge and rock."

Alice in Chains. Alice in Spencerland. Now I wasn't sure which nickname fit her better. I thought they both sounded disturbingly sexy.

She placed the squeaky truck back on the table. "I've never met my dad's family. He was originally from a small town in Washington. His parents are gone, but his brothers and sisters are still there. Just this year, I started reaching out to them on social media. It's been nice having an online rapport with them."

Immersed in what felt like an emotional moment, I said, "Someday I might try to find my dad."

"Really?" Her gaze locked onto mine. "How would you go about doing something like that?"

"I could submit my DNA on the ancestry sites that help you search for biological family members."

"I think that's a great idea."

"You do?"

"Absolutely." She stepped closer to me. "You have a right to know who your dad is."

"Yeah, but I probably won't get any hits, anyway. How likely is it that my father or someone from his family would've submitted their DNA? And even if by some miracle I do locate him, he might not want anything to do with me." I'd already been cast aside by my aunt and uncle. I didn't want to pin my hopes on a stranger, too. "When I was a kid, I spent a lot of time imagining what he would be like, but that doesn't mean he's going to live up to my expectations."

"I have expectations about who my future husband is supposed to be. And I'm not going to give up on finding him."

"We could both end up being disillusioned."

"I hope not." She moved away from me.

"Yeah, me, too." I kept opening myself up to her, sharing my insecurities, saying things I never intended to say. "Are we done? Can I change out of this shirt now?"

"Certainly."

"I left my T-shirt in the bedroom. You can come along, if you want to. To give Cookie and Candy their toys," I clarified. I wasn't inviting her for any other reason.

"Are they hiding under the bed again?"

"Yes. But I think they'll come out to snag their toys and sneak another peek at you."

Alice joined me in my bedroom. I removed the red shirt and yanked my T-shirt back over my head.

"Should I put the toys on the floor?" she asked.

"Sure, just set them down."

She placed them near her feet. The bait worked. The dogs came creeping out. They looked at me to get my approval. I nodded and said, "Have at it, girls."

They each grabbed a toy and started chewing the rubber. The squeaking noise was deafening.

Alice laughed in sheer delight, and I smiled, too.

"They're so cute," she said, bouncing on her heels. "Did they pick the right ones?"

"No. But they'll swap at some point."

"I can barely tell them apart. They look like twins."

"Cookie's ear is a little tweaked from her injury, and Candy is a little fluffier."

She studied the dogs. "Oh, yes, I see that now. My niece and nephew are twins, but it's easy to tell them apart."

I stated the obvious. "Because of their gender differences?"

She laughed again. "Yes, but their personalities are different, too. My nephew is wonderfully behaved."

"And your niece is a hellion?" I lifted my eyebrows. "Like her auntie?"

"Who me?" She made an innocent expression, putting her hands beneath her chin and batting her lashes. "I had nothing to do with it."

"Yeah, I can see how sweet you are." Little vixen that she was. "The twins are cute kids. I've never met them, but Kirby shows me pictures of them all the time. He's an adoring grandpa."

"It's nice that you think the twins are cute. But

I'd rather that you left Kirby out of it." She grabbed the shirt I discarded. "I know he dotes on the kids. I hear about it from Mary all the time. I don't need you singing his praises, too."

"At least Kirby is a real person. It's better than you talking about a fictional husband you might never even meet," I snapped.

She glared at me. "That's a low blow."

Okay, so she was right. It wasn't fair for me to squelch her dreams. But her attitude annoyed me. "You can't get mad every time I say something decent about Kirby."

She huffed out a breath. There was no reasoning with her when it came to Kirby. We could argue about this until we were blue in the face, and never get anywhere.

I tried to make nice by asking, "Do you have your wedding all planned out? You know, the details women sometimes think about?"

She jerked her head. "No."

I didn't believe her. I inched forward, showing as much interest as I could. "Not even a little?"

"Maybe," she conceded.

"Come on. Tell me what parts you've thought about."

She hesitated, as if she didn't quite trust me with the information. But she gave in and said, "I want a black diamond for my engagement ring."

"Really?" I was surprised by her choice. It seemed a little gloomy to me. "Why?"

"I like how unconventional they are. Besides, black diamonds represent strength and power."

Now that I had time to reconsider her jewelry preference, I was intrigued by it. "That is kind of cool."

She fussed with the shirt in her hand. "I haven't picked out the type of dress I want. I don't want to go overboard when I don't even have a groom yet."

"You've got plenty of time for that." I glanced at the dogs and realized that they'd stopped squeaking their toys. Did they sense that Alice and I were discussing something important to her? Something that was totally foreign to me?

I knew nothing about weddings. Or phantom husbands. Or wannabe wives. I couldn't fathom spending eternity with someone. I was just trying to get through each day.

"How many more fittings do you think we're going to have?" I asked, changing the subject.

"It depends on my next shopping excursion." She seemed to be studying me now. "Would you rather I make fewer trips over here?"

"No, it's fine. You can come by however often you need to. But maybe we could do one of the fittings at your place."

She gave me a weird look. "Why do you want to do that?"

"Because you never asked me to come over before, and that always made me feel a little slighted. But you can make up for it now." I chanced a half-cocked grin, using what little charm I had left. "You can cook me dinner or something."

She rolled her eyes. "Are you seriously trying to beg a home-cooked meal off of me?"

"I seem to recall you telling me that you liked to cook."

"I do," she said, making me wonder if she just might do it.

I never really knew with Alice. She was a hard nut to crack. This woman from my past, invading my mind and disorganizing my life. I was suffering just by being in her company. But that didn't stop me from wanting to spend more time with her—in whatever troubling ways I could.

Five

Alice

I invited Spencer to my home for the final fitting. For the past few weeks, I'd been going to his house and working out the wardrobe with him. But now, at the very end, he was coming to me. He wanted to see my place, so I caved in. I was cooking dinner for him, too.

To keep the evening from seeming romantic, I asked him to bring the dogs. By now, Candy and Cookie had become accustomed to me, so I figured they would be comfortable here. Spencer was also bringing Pete, per my request. The more company, the better.

Much to my dismay, I thought about Spencer day and night. I touched myself in the shower and imagined his hands on me. I rolled around in bed and fantasized that he was deep inside me. I did all of the breathless things that women did when they were consumed with a man.

I shook away those feelings and focused on the Mexican-style coleslaw on the counter in front of me. I made it look festive, with red and green cabbage, fresh corn directly from the cob, black beans and diced peppers. For the main course, a tamale casserole was bubbling in the oven. A pan of Spanish rice simmered on the stove, too.

Spencer was due any minute. I'd changed my clothes twice already, finally settling on a lace-trimmed camisole, a lightweight printed shrug, skinny white jeans and pink cowboy boots.

When the doorbell rang, my heart leaped to my throat, and I rushed to answer it. All three dogs were on leashes. Candy and Cookie took ladylike steps into my condo. The bulldog was his usual self, engine revved and ready to go.

Spencer held a bouquet of pink carnations in his other hand. He smiled at me. "These are from Pete."

"Thank you. They're lovely." I took the flowers. The dog was already slobbering at my feet.

"I guess we chose the right color," Spencer said.

I assumed he meant the carnations and how they matched my boots. "Yes, you did." It was cute how he'd said "we" as if the dog had actually had been involved. But it was weird, too, because it was the first time Spencer had given me flowers. I wasn't sure how to feel about that.

"You look pretty, Alice."

"You look great, too." He was as handsome as ever, in a slim black T-shirt, fitted jeans and black roper boots, scuffed at the toes. "I'll put these in water."

He let the dogs off their leashes, and man and animals followed me into the kitchen.

"Dinner will be ready soon." I filled a vase and arranged the flowers. I petted the dogs and put a water bowl on the floor for them. "I thought we could eat on the patio since the weather is so nice tonight."

"It smells wonderful." Spencer stood near the stove. He lifted the lid on the rice. "It looks good, too." He glanced up at me. "Remember when I used to live on frozen pizza?"

Now I had visions of his old apartment and eating those pizzas in bed with him. "Yes, I remember." Every memory that pertained to him involved sex, or post sex, or something I would be smart to forget. I wished he hadn't brought it up. But what else were we supposed to reminiscence about?

"I still keep my favorite brand around for when I need a junk food fix."

I agonized over the deliberate way he was looking at me. "The messy kind with the cheese-stuffed crust?"

"Yeah." He broke eye contact. "I cook a little now." He checked out the slaw I'd left on the counter. "Not like this, though."

I redirected the conversation. "Do you want to see the rest of my place?" My condo consisted of an ultramodern living room, a cozy den, two spacious bedrooms and two full baths.

He nodded, and I gave him a tour, with the dogs following along, their little paws tapping on the hardwood floors.

Spencer seemed intrigued by my bedroom. He glanced around, taking it all in. I'd decorated in jewel tones, with lots of shiny knickknacks. The bed was crisply made, showing no signs of my restless nights. I'd made sure of it.

"As you can see, I set up your wardrobe in here." The clothes I'd purchased for him hung on a rolling rack, and his shoes and accessories were stacked in clear plastic boxes. "I figured you can use my bathroom to change."

"Whatever works." He glanced around again. "I expected your room to be messier."

"You thought I'd be a slob?"

"No, just that things would be scattered about."

I pulled a guilty face. "Actually, I cleaned up today since you were coming over. Normally I am on the messier side."

"Then I had you pegged right."

"Yes, I guess you did." I sometimes left my bras and panties on the floor, but I wasn't going to tell him that. "Did you bring the rest of your stuff for the fitting?" I asked. "Your jeans, boots and jacket that we'll be using?" He was responsible for providing those items.

"They're in my truck. I'll get them later, after dinner."

"Then let's eat." By now, I knew the food would be ready.

We returned to the kitchen, and I removed the

casserole from the oven. I filled our plates, and he helped me carry them outside, along with a pitcher of sweet tea.

We sat at a glass-topped table. My patio offered brick pavers, a built-in barbecue and a fire ring, set amid leafy plants and a fragrant herb garden. The dogs made themselves at home, lolling on the pavement and enjoying the chew sticks Spencer had brought for them.

"You have a nice yard," he said.

"Thank you. I rented this condo when I first got my share of the money from Mama's songs."

He motioned to the windchimes hanging from a wooden post. "Those are a great touch. They're beautifully tuned," he added, as a light breeze stirred them.

Curious to know more about his creative side, I asked, "What made you want to be become a songwriter?" I'd never questioned him about his goals and dreams in the past. But he was always so reluctant to talk about himself then, he probably wouldn't have told me, anyway.

He swigged his tea. Was he gathering his thoughts?

Finally, he put down his glass and said, "I've always been good at writing, at putting words together. It was one of my outlets when I was growing up. I used to write short stories and poems. My writing got pretty dark after my mom died. Sometimes it still is."

I nodded. He'd become known for penning the lyrics to some very famous, very tragic songs. "Do you sing fairly well? My mother used to say that it helped if songwriters could sing their own songs."

"I wouldn't be able to make my living as a vocalist, but I sing well enough to make my own demos."

"What about the actual music part?" People in the industry praised him for being a brilliant composer. "How did that come about?"

"My aunt and uncle forced me to take piano lessons." He scooped up some of the casserole. "I hated it in the beginning. My teacher was brutal, and my aunt and uncle made it feel like punishment."

"Were you being classically trained? Chopin and Bach and all of that?"

He ate the food on his fork, then replied, "Yes, but classically trained doesn't just mean the type of music you're taught to play, it's technique, too. And I was good at it, really, really good. So good, my teacher was trying to prepare me for a music conservatory. She told my aunt and uncle that I could have a career as a concert pianist, if I put my heart and mind to it."

I tried to envision him, young and troubled, being forced to do something he didn't want to do. "How old were you when you first started to play? When the lessons began?"

"Eleven. I appreciate the classics now. But back then, they were torture."

"When did you change your style?"

"When I was fourteen, I saw a movie about Jerry Lee Lewis. And that was it for me. I started playing old rockabilly tunes. I loved the sound, but I was also doing it to piss off my aunt and uncle." He laughed a little. "I'd pound out those songs first thing in the morning, giving them a whole lotta shakin' going on."

I laughed, too. "And hence your days of being a bad boy began."

"Yeah, but it wasn't just about being bad. I was trying to soothe my soul, too."

I gently asked, "When did the drinking start?"

"It was around the same time. But even before that, I used to watch my aunt and uncle mix their favorite nightcaps. When I finally got the urge to try it, it became easy for me to raid their liquor cabinet. I only did it a little at first, though." He paused. "Then a lot later on."

"I guess it makes sense that you became a bartender, since you grew up in a house where cocktails were being served."

"I suppose so. When I turned eighteen and moved here to Nashville, I got a job as a barback in a restaurant. Then later, I started tending bar at the club where I met you in person for the first time."

I didn't respond. I didn't want to talk about that night or how sinful it was. I ached in all the wrong places just thinking about it.

As Spencer fell silent, I watched him eat. He mixed up everything on his plate, whereas I was keeping each dish separate. Was I trying to control my urges, even with my food? Normally I did what he was doing, letting the flavors seep together.

Before things turned too quiet, I said, "I got ice cream for dessert. I'm not a baker. My sister is a pastry chef, but I'm no good at it."

"Ice cream works for me. What flavor did you get?"

"I got two. Banana chocolate chip and cookies and cream."

He smiled. "Then I'll take some of each."

"That's what I plan to do, too." His laid-back, sexy smile was making me weak. Everything about him was dragging me under his spell, just like last time.

We finished dinner and cleared the dishes, taking them inside. The dogs didn't follow us. They stayed on the patio, but I left the sliding glass door open for them.

I served the ice cream in the living room, placing our bowls on the coffee table and offering Spencer a seat on the sofa. Before I sat down, I streamed some music, and he grinned when "Great Balls of Fire" started to play. It was the title song for the Jerry Lee Lewis movie he'd mentioned earlier.

"Great choice," he said.

I joined him on the sofa. "I aim to please." But not too much, I thought. I wasn't supposed to be thinking about pleasing him in other ways.

"Will we be listening to any of Kirby's songs tonight?" he asked.

"Not a chance," I replied.

"Not even the songs I wrote for him?"

"Nope. I'm afraid not." I dipped into my bowl. In some way or another, he always managed to bring Kirby into it.

"I wonder if they'll ever make a movie about his life."

I heaved a sigh. "They probably will when he's dead and gone. Or maybe they'll do it before. As arrogant as he is, he's probably shopping his book for movie deals as we speak."

"He stayed with me when I was going through withdrawals. He took care of me the entire time."

I tried to picture Kirby as Spencer's nursemaid, but it was tough for me to see him in that role. "Was it really bad?" I'd heard that alcohol withdrawal could be serious.

"It sure as hell felt bad to me. I had the shakes something awful." He held out his hand as if to check his steadiness now. "I was sweating and sick, you know, the whole shebang. It comes in stages, and it seemed like it was never going to end."

"How long did it last?"

"About a week."

"You mentioned before that you're involved in an outpatient program, but couldn't you have checked into a treatment center, instead of having Kirby stay with you?"

"Going to a place like that would have made me feel trapped. And I like that Kirby took care of me. He made me feel valued. He still does."

"It's weird that the man who helped you is the same man who destroyed my childhood. Don't you think there's a warped sort of irony in that?"

"I don't know. I guess." He shifted beside me. "Maybe I should get my stuff out of the truck now so we can do the fitting."

"That's probably a good idea." We were both done with our ice cream, and I didn't want to keep talking about Kirby.

He got up and left, and I shut off the music. The dogs came inside. Cookie looked around for Spencer and started to whine.

"It's okay," I said to her. "He's coming right back."

She kept whining, so I picked her up, hoping to comfort her. But then Candy and Pete pawed at me, wanting affection, too. I sat on the floor and let all of them climb onto my lap.

Spencer returned and marveled at the sight. "Look at you."

"What can I say? I'm the new dog whisperer." Cookie remained with me, even though her beloved owner was back. Candy and Pete stayed put, too, determined to keep me close.

"More like the new dog spoiler. I should have hired you to be their stylist, too. You could put them in ribbons and bows. Or leather jackets or whatever."

I got up off the floor. "I think I better stick to getting you ready for your shoot."

He nodded. "Yes, ma'am."

We went to my room so he could try everything on. The dogs came with us, finding cozy spots to relax.

The fitting went well, with Spencer standing in front of my closet door mirror while I checked each outfit. But when we took a break, he sat on the edge of my bed, and the moment turned painfully intimate. He looked so big and broad, wrinkling a delicate corner of my bedspread.

"There's supposed to be a makeup and hair person on the shoot," he said.

I tugged at the edge of my camisole. "I assumed

there would be. I was going to talk to them about tousling your hair for the rebel looks I created."

"I'd rather do it myself." He stood and moved away from my bed. "Or let you do it."

"I guess we'll see how it goes." For now, I was just trying to keep my perspective. "You need to change for me one more time." I gestured to the final outfit.

He grabbed everything and went into my bathroom.

I glanced at the dogs while I waited. Pete was leaning against a decorative pillow that was propped in a corner, using it as a cushion. The girls were curled up next to him. All three were fast asleep.

Spencer returned. The last ensemble was sporty: a plaid shirt, cargo pants and brown chukka boots. It was perfect on him. But everything was. I came up beside him, so that both of us were reflected in the mirror.

"Do you need to make any modifications?" he asked.

I gazed at him in the glass. "I got a beanie to go with it, but it's up to you if you want to wear it."

"Can I see it?"

I removed the knit cap from its labeled box and gave it to him.

He tried it on. "If they do any pictures outdoors, I could wear it for that."

I adjusted the cap a little lower on his head. "I like it this way better."

"Yeah, but don't pull it down over my eyes. Or I won't be able to see how sexy you are."

"You shouldn't be looking at me that way, any-way." But it was too late. He already was.

He reached out to skim his thumb across my cheek, and I leaned into him, my mind spinning like a pin-wheel. He moved closer, making me even dizzier.

We nearly kissed, until I came to my senses and pulled back. My hand slipped, knocking the beanie off his head.

"Sorry," we both said at the same time. A mutual apology, for a shared mistake of getting too close.

He crammed his hands in his pockets, as if he didn't know what else to do with them. I didn't know what to do, either. If we'd kissed for real, what would have happened afterwards? More kisses? A desper-ate night of forbidden sex?

He frowned. "I wish I wasn't so damned attracted to you."

"I'm feeling the same. It's torture." My pulse pounded, between my legs, where I wanted him most. I even pressed my thighs together.

A muscle flexed in his jaw. "I'm not going to sleep for shit tonight."

"I've barely slept since we've gotten to know each other again." I picked up the beanie off the floor, returning it to its box. "But what do two celibate people know? We're probably making more out of it than it is."

"I hope so." He shifted his stance. "But I should go now."

He headed to the bathroom to change into his regular clothes, and I leaned against my dresser, struggling to breathe.

While I was still dragging air into my lungs, he emerged and handed me the outfit he'd removed. I hung everything on the rack, and he woke up the dogs.

We went into the living room, and he gathered the leashes. Once the animals were secure, we all stood at the front door.

The shoot was a few days away. Then this job would be over, and I wouldn't have to see Spencer again. But how was I supposed to cope with my feelings until then?

He thanked me for dinner, and we said an awkward goodbye. He left, the dogs falling into step with him.

After I shut and locked the door, I returned to my bedroom to reorganize his wardrobe. But handling his clothes only intensified my unfulfilled ache. As I smoothed the pants he'd just worn, running my hands along the fabric, I closed my eyes.

And imagined that I was touching him instead.

Six

Alice

On the day of the photo shoot, I did whatever I could to impress Derek Jordon, the world-renowned photographer I'd been so eager to work with. Thankfully, he loved all of the looks I'd created. But I didn't want to get overly confident.

Derek was a perfectionist, with his own unique sense of style. He sported a shaved head and a nose ring. The hair and makeup person, a chipper brunette named Nellie, was his college-aged daughter.

Spencer asked her if I could style his hair for the rebel pics. Even after our close encounter at my condo the other night, he still wanted me to do that. Nellie was agreeable. She backed away, letting me handle it alone.

Spencer settled into a director's-style chair in the dining room, which was where Nellie had set up her kits and portable mirror. I intended to work from behind him, looking into the mirror, but he invited me to stand between his legs. He made room for me, and I moved into place, facing him, with my heart thumping in my chest.

I used a dollop of gel and ran my hands through his thick dark locks, tousling each strand just so.

"Are you enjoying this?" I asked.

"This?" he replied, his gaze roaming over me.

"The shoot," I clarified. I wasn't referring to me doing his hair.

"Yeah, it's been fun so far." He was still looking too closely at me.

I sucked in my breath. "Candy and Cookie did well." The dogs had already been in a couple of pictures with him. They were at the rescue now, to keep them from getting underfoot. But they were the least of my worries.

I finished his hair, but I didn't want to stop touching him. I glanced toward the living room, reminding myself of the importance of this job. "You should go. Derek has the next shot lined up."

"Are my clothes okay?"

"You look great." I loosened his tie a bit more. "But you really should go."

"You need to *let* me go, Alice."

I didn't understand what he meant. Then I realized

that I was still standing between his legs. I mumbled an apology and stepped out of his way.

Mercy me.

Spencer rose from his chair, and I watched him pose for the next round of pictures. With the shadows playing across his face, he was a sight to behold. I could've drooled all over myself, especially when Derek had him straddling his piano bench.

Spencer's shirtsleeves were rolled up, exposing part of his tattoo. I could tell that Derek was fascinated with it. Soon, he asked Spencer to change into a tank top so he could photograph the tattoo in its entirety. Spencer made the switch, and his body art became a focal point. Derek used diffuser boxes to light it, making the details more pronounced.

Following the tattoo pics, we broke for lunch. While we ate, Derek and I talked shop, Nellie texted her boyfriend and Spencer listened to music with headphones on.

After lunch and a wardrobe change, we moved to the garage. In this setting, Derek shot Spencer in his biker gear, using his Harley as a prop. Spencer caught my gaze from across the garage, leaving me in a rush of unwelcome heat. He looked damn fine, perched on his shiny new bike. All that chrome, all that male muscle.

Trying to distract myself, I shifted my gaze to Nellie. But that didn't help. She smiled and winked, letting me know that she was wise to what was going on. Apparently, she could tell that Spencer and I were hot for each other. By now, I figured that Derek knew, too, and had been channeling Spencer's desire for me into the shoot. I could only imagine how sexy the pictures were going to be.

Derek took the final ones outdoors on the lawn. Spencer wore the plaid shirt and cargo pants for those. Rain was in the forecast, and Derek was hoping for a downpour. He wanted to catch Spencer in it.

I provided disposable rain slickers for Derek, Nellie and me, in case we needed them. Spencer didn't get one.

When it started sprinkling, he crammed the beanie on his head, and Derek caught some candid poses.

The rain intensified, and the photographer got the shots he'd been hoping for. I adjusted the hood on my slicker and stared lustfully at Spencer. He was getting drenched, his shirt clinging to his skin.

A short time later, it was over. While Spencer changed into dry clothes, Derek and Nellie packed up their gear. I exchanged business cards with them, and Derek and I agreed to stay in touch. Apparently, I'd made a positive impression and now had the important industry contact I'd hoped for.

After father and daughter were gone, I stayed to wrap things up with Spencer, helping him put away the wardrobe.

"I can wash your wet clothes," I said, still acting as his stylist. "Or take them to a service, if you prefer."

"That's okay. I'll wash them later. For now, I just threw them on top of the dryer."

"Well, you certainly nailed every shot." I was genuinely impressed with his modeling skills.

"I couldn't have done it without you. It really helped having you here."

"I'm glad you think so." Should I head home now? Or keep finding things to talk about? Clearly, I was struggling to leave. I glanced down at the floor. Now I wished that we would've kissed at my condo. At least then, if I never saw him again, I would have a memory of a recent kiss.

"Do you want some hot chocolate?" he asked.

I lifted my gaze. "That sounds nice." I was glad that he'd offered me a legitimate reason to stay. But the urge to kiss him hadn't gone away, and that was dangerous.

I followed him to the kitchen, and he poured the instant packets into our cups and heated the water in the microwave.

Neither of us spoke. It was still raining outside and I could hear it beating against the roof.

When the hot chocolate was ready, we drank it where we were, standing at the counter.

"Are you hungry?" he asked.

For food, no. For him, yes. I waited an anxious beat before I replied, "I'm still full from lunch. But if you want to eat, go ahead."

He shook his head. "I'm full, too. I was just checking on you."

Suddenly I couldn't take it anymore. I said what was on my mind. "We should have kissed when we had the chance."

His gaze locked onto mine. "We still can."

I moistened my lips, eager, excited, but painfully

cautious, too. "Just one kiss, just to see what it feels like again."

"Whatever you want, Alice. Whatever you think is best." He set his cup down. "But let's try to make it count, okay?"

I put down my drink and took a step in his direction. A part of me wanted to turn tail and run, afraid that one kiss would never be enough. He watched me, anticipation in his eyes.

Once I was upon him, I lifted my face to his. I reached for him, getting ready. He leaned forward, and I pressed my lips to his. He tasted like chocolate and marshmallows, but I probably did, too. The two of us, warm and sweet.

He wrapped me in his arms, and our tongues met and mated.

Were we making it count? Was this the kiss we'd both been waiting for? Not by a long shot, I thought.

"More," I whispered, against his mouth. "More."

He cupped my ass and dragged me against his fly. I relished his hardness. My softness. The godawful hunger.

I wanted him beyond reason. Beyond logic. Beyond everything that was keeping me on the sexual straight and narrow. Forget Mr. Right. I would find him later. For now, there was only Spencer.

He deepened the kiss, and I made up my mind, dangerous as it was. I was going to sleep with him, here and now.

I pulled back and asked, "Do you have protection?"

He stared at me, as if my words didn't quite register. Or maybe he was just trying to remember if he had condoms. I searched his gaze, antsy for his reply. I needed to get him out of my system, out of my blood, but I couldn't forgo the protection.

He said, "They're in the bottom of my dresser, with some old clothes I never wear. But I hope they're still good."

I reached for his hand and shivered from the feeling. "Let's go find out."

He threaded his fingers through mine and led me to his bedroom. I stood off to the side while he retrieved the condoms. He checked the expiration date on the box.

My heart pounded. "Are they okay?"

He nodded. "We'll be safe."

I sighed in relief, and he pulled off his T-shirt. He was already barefoot. All that was left were his pants. I was wearing a lot more clothes than he was.

He gestured for me to remove something of mine, and I slipped out of my boots and peeled off my socks. But I didn't go any further. I couldn't seem to manage it, not with how shaky I was beginning to feel.

"What's wrong?" he asked.

"I'm actually a little scared." The five years I'd been alone seemed like an eternity now.

"We don't have to do this if it's too much for you." He spoke gently, reminding me that I was in charge, that this was my choice.

"But I want to be with you." The need was too great to walk away, even if I was nervous.

"Maybe I can help you relax."

"I'd like that." I wanted him to make it easier somehow.

He approached me, and I looked up at him, captivated by the handsome angles of his face. He kissed me, and the kiss was much softer than the one in the kitchen. I rocked forward. No one had ever been protective of me before, and especially not him.

He whispered in my ear, "Can I undress you?"

I gave him permission, and he divested me of my blouse and bra. As he thumbed my nipples, I swayed on my feet.

"You're perfect," he said. "But you always were."

I had small, perky breasts and pointy pink nipples. He leaned down to take one of them into his mouth, and I cupped the back of his head.

Back and forth he went, from one of my breasts to the other, licking and sucking. He undid my jeans and slid his hand down the front of my panties. He applied silky pressure, working his fingers in tiny circles.

I gripped his shoulders. Nothing had ever felt so good. Yet I knew it was only going to get better. He continued to tease me, to arouse me, to make my head spin.

I came, slick and warm, with him touching me that way.

After it was over, he helped me out of my jeans, peeling my panties off with them. I stood naked before him, and he scooped me up and carried me to bed.

He leaned over me, and I tugged him down. I

opened his jeans and put my hand inside his boxers. I felt him up, just as he'd done to me.

He groaned in satisfaction, and all too soon, he was naked and fully aroused. He put on a condom and braced himself above me. Eager for his penetration, I parted my thighs.

He entered me, and we moved in unison, in a rhythm that came naturally. No words were exchanged, only moans and murmurs and rough sounds of pleasure. He lifted my legs and pulled them higher and tighter around his body. Good thing I was bendy like that. He was agile, too, and with muscles to die for. I skimmed a hand down his abs, feeling them ripple.

We kissed, tongues tangling, teeth clashing. Together we were lethal, fast and furious, wild and desperate.

I dug my nails into his shoulders, and he thrust even harder and deeper, pushing both of us toward completion.

I didn't need any extra stimulation. Just having him inside me, moving like a maniac was enough. I came in convulsive waves, drowning in my own sticky wetness.

He arched like an animal, rearing up during his orgasm. I watched him, thinking how magnificently primal he was.

He collapsed on top of me, and neither of us moved. Finally, he lifted his head and peeked at me through one eye. The other eye was covered by his free-falling hair.

He rolled off of me, but he stayed close, holding me, making me sigh. Feeling the almighty afterglow, I curled up against him, letting the sensation engulf me. I wanted it to last, but before I got too accustomed to it, I eased away from him.

Silence hovered in the air. He seemed confused that I ended it so soon. But as comforting as it felt, as much as I liked it, I feared that I might get attached to him.

My old lover. My new lover. Were we back to having an affair? The thought both scared and excited me.

Spencer frowned, almost as if he was trying to read my mind.

"Is the offer to eat still good?" I asked, creating a diversion. I didn't want him to figure me out.

"You worked up an appetite?" Now he seemed amused.

I fluttered my mascara-spiked lashes, playing the femme fatale, keeping him distracted. "Sex can be hard work."

"The hardest." He glanced down at himself. He was still wearing the condom. "I better go get rid of this. Meet me in the kitchen?"

"Okay." I got out of bed. He did, too, but before he headed for the bathroom, he kissed me, making me long for the afterglow again.

We separated, and I got haphazardly dressed, wearing only my blouse and panties.

I entered the kitchen and opened Spencer's fridge. I spotted an assortment of deli meats, along with eggs and cheese and other basics. I checked the freezer and uncovered a stack of the frozen pizzas he favored. Then, as I stood there, staring into the freezer's chilly abyss, I heard his footsteps behind me.

I spun around. He was attired in his underwear, looking rough and messy, like the bad boy he used to be. Was sleeping with him a mistake? Had I acted too impulsively?

"What do you want to make?" he asked.

I removed one of the pizzas. "How about your old standby?"

"That works for me." He preheated the oven, setting the digital dial. "I'm going to have a ginger ale now. They've become my go-to since I got sober. Do you want one?"

I nodded. Anything to keep myself busy.

He went to the mini fridge in the bar where he kept the sodas. He returned with two chilled cans. He handed me mine, and I opened the tab and took a hasty drink.

"Are you having second thoughts?" he asked.

"About what?" I responded inanely. I knew what he meant, but I didn't want to seem too obvious, even if he'd managed to figure me out.

"About us." He studied me. "Are you having buyer's remorse?"

I looked past him, landing my sights on the kitchen window. The glass was fogged, misty and gray. "I didn't buy anything," I replied, returning my gaze to his.

"You gave up your celibacy. That's a big buy-in after five years." He pulled a hand through his already messy hair. "I'm sorry if I'm not the right guy for you."

"You have nothing to be sorry for." It was just sex, I reminded myself, but with some sweetness tossed in. "It was nice being back in your bed. It's what I wanted, what I needed."

He swigged his soda with a noisy swallow. "Then do you want to keep doing it?"

I should have said no. That this was the only time we would be together. But I couldn't bear to let him go this soon. "Maybe for a little while."

"A little while is all I have to give, Alice."

"I know." And that was all I needed from him, I decided. No more. No less. I couldn't keep worrying about getting attached, either. I had to release that fear.

He came forward and wrapped me in his arms. He was getting adept at cuddling. He nuzzled the top of my head and said, "I think you're going to become my muse."

I stepped back, needing to look at him, to see the usual darkness in his eyes. "Have you ever had a muse before?"

"No, but I like the idea. Don't you?"

"It could be interesting." Some of the most beautiful songs in the world were inspired by real live muses. But some of the most troubling were, too. It went both ways.

The oven beeped, reaching the desired temperature. I'd almost forgotten about the pizza. But now I was grateful for the reprieve. I didn't want to think too deeply about being Spencer's muse.

Thirty minutes later, Spencer piled the pizza onto paper plates, giving us each three ginormous pieces.

"Let's pig out in bed," he said. "Like we used to."

I didn't protest. Eating in bed with him was a naughty memory I didn't mind repeating. Besides, I was trying to relax and not keep stressing about everything. For now, there was nothing wrong with being his lover, or his muse.

We retreated to his room, sat cross-legged amid the rumpled covers and feasted on our meal, with a stack of napkins nearby.

"It's hard to imagine you growing up so rich," I said. "Especially while you're gnawing your way through frozen pizza."

He chewed and swallowed. "It's not frozen anymore."

"You know what I mean." He was already on his second slice.

He shrugged. "When I lived with my aunt and uncle, we had a personal chef who made all of our meals. I wasn't allowed to have junk like this."

"Then it stands to reason why you enjoy it so much."

He tore at the cheese-stuffed crust, pulling it apart and making the mozzarella seep out. "Robert and Roberta wouldn't be pleased."

"Those are your aunt's and uncle's names?" I burst into a laugh. "Seriously?"

He laughed, as well. "He goes by Rob and she goes

by Bobbie. But it's still annoying how alike they are, right down to their names."

I popped a piece of pepperoni into my mouth. The pizza was loaded with them. "Did you have a nanny?"

"Yes, but she wasn't very nice. Bobbie hired someone who ruled with an iron fist, and Rob thoroughly approved. Eventually I got too old for a nanny, so she went off to discipline some other poor kid, I guess."

"Your aunt and uncle sound wretched." That was the only way I could think to describe them. "They could have at least hired Nanny McPhee or Mary Poppins or someone who could've protected you."

"Yeah, don't I wish. It's weird, the relationship my mom had with my aunt. They didn't get along worth a damn, but they still saw each other all the time. Bobbie was always pressuring Mom to give up her acting dreams. The fact that Mom used to borrow money from Bobbie didn't help. My aunt liked to throw that in my face. How irresponsible she thought my mom was. How our rent would've never gotten paid if it hadn't been for her."

"That's a terrible thing to say to a child." The way they'd treated him was deplorable.

"I think my mom would've been a successful actress, if she'd lived to see it through. She never did any TV or movies, but she was studying her craft and working toward the future." He ate the gooey crust he'd pulled apart. "She did mostly corporate stuff, like job-training videos. Her favorite one was for a bank, where she got to play a teller who was being robbed. When she rehearsed it at home, she let me pretend to be the robber."

I couldn't help but smile. I envisioned him with a bandit mask over his eyes. "What about the department store work? Wasn't that enough to pay the rent?"

"The perfume gigs? That was freelance. She tried to keep her schedule open for auditions. When she didn't have a babysitter for me, she would take me along."

I liked the way he spoke of her, the loving tone in his voice. "What was her name?"

"Lynnette." He reached for a napkin and handed me one, too. "I know that your mom's name was Cathy Birch. I saw her songwriting credits. Was Birch her maiden name?"

"Yes. She and my dad were never married. They just lived together and had us kids. That always bothered me."

"Them not being married? Why? It was still a committed relationship, wasn't it?"

"Yes, but Mama wanted him to marry her. She used to say how it made her sad that he didn't believe in marriage."

"Maybe that's why marriage is so important to you now."

"Maybe." To stop him from delving deeper into how badly I wanted a husband, I said, "Wait until your aunt and uncle see the photo spread of you, looking all badass and beautiful. You should send them a signed copy."

"Badass and beautiful?" He laughed. "I hope that

isn't how the magazine describes me." He leaned closer to me. "Now you...you're the beautiful one."

Fueled by his compliment, I kissed him. He pulled me onto his lap, rubbed against me and made both of us moan.

All over again.

Seven

Spencer

Alice and I rolled over the bed, knocking our plates and leftover food onto the floor.

I tore open her blouse, the buttons popping. Immediately realizing what I'd done, I cursed to myself and said, "Sorry. I'll get you another one." I would buy her anything she wanted.

"It doesn't matter." She ran her nails down the front of my body, leaving scratch marks on my chest and stomach.

I went after her panties, practically tearing them off, too. Then I gripped both of her wrists, held her hands above her head and kissed her soft and slow, bringing the frenzy to a halt. She stopped thrashing and sighed against my lips.

After the kiss, I looked down at her. She was looking up at me, too, waiting to see what came next. I was still holding her hands above her head.

I released my hold on her and said, "I need your permission."

"For what?" she asked, blinking at me.

"To go down on you." I wanted to hear her tell me to do it. I leaned forward and whispered, "Will you let me?"

"Yes," she replied. "Do it." She was already arching her hips in anticipation. "You were always so good at it."

"I still am." Or I sure as hell intended to be. I worked my way down, breathing against her skin. I paused purposely at her navel, teasing her, making her wait.

She pushed her hands into my hair. "You're probably going to haunt my dreams."

"Just the erotic ones, I hope."

"Definitely." She arched her hips again, her hands still tunneled into my hair.

I put my face between her legs. She was smooth, fully waxed, and I parted her with my thumbs. I used my tongue, swirling, licking, making her half-mad.

I could feel her excitement, her honey-slick moisture, her sensual shivers. She kept moving closer to my mouth, making me aroused, too.

When she came, her entire body quavered, and I continued my foray, absorbing every last shudder.

I raised my head and kissed her, slipping my tongue past her lips. She pressed against me, and I got even harder.

She was already naked, and I was nearly there. I removed my boxers, tore open a condom and put it on as quickly as I could.

I positioned her on top, and she arched her glorious body. Cloudy light spilled in from the French doors, bathing her in a hazy glow.

I circled her waist with my hands, and she impaled herself, riding me into the kingdom of heaven—or the depths of hell—in furious pursuit of whatever this hungry sensation was. She moved slowly, taking me inch by inch. I groaned my approval, watching her hips rise and fall. She increased the tempo, taking us both to new heights.

Was her heart beating at a runaway pace? Mine was, in every pulse point of my body. I missed this feeling. I missed having sex. And she was making it so damned good. She adjusted herself on my lap, creating deeper friction.

My vision blurred; my muscles tensed; my mind slipped into caveman mode. I wanted to hang on, to let the thrill last. But I was too far gone. I gave up the fight and let myself fall, coming strong and fast.

I went into the bathroom, came back, put my boxers on and cleaned up the pizza off the floor. Alice offered to help, but I told to her stay put. I liked how cozy she looked in my bed.

I rejoined her, getting under the covers. I took her

in my arms, doing the romantic thing, or trying to. It was still new to me.

She made a dreamy sound and put her head against my chest, so I figured I must be doing it right.

I wasn't sure what to expect from this affair. Was it going to be sex-only again? Or would we go on some actual dates? I was scheduled for a business trip next week, and now I was thinking of asking her to join me. But this didn't seem like the time to broach the subject, so I just held her instead.

To keep myself occupied, I played with the spiky tips of her hair. I'd seen it brushed flat before, but mostly it was stiff and pointy.

"What color is it for real?" I asked.

She stirred in my arms. "What?"

"Your hair."

"It's blond, but I bleach it to make it whiter."

"I'm glad you're still wearing it this way. I always liked how retro it seemed, like Billy Idol or something."

She moved onto her side. "Didn't I ever tell you that 'Rebel Yell' was my karaoke song?"

I chuckled at her expression; she was shooting me an Idol-type snarl. "No, I don't recall you ever saying that. But I remember that you used to listen to early punk."

"It was the fashions that first caught my attention, pictures of people in the seventies and eighties, with their tough and trashed clothes. I was especially interested in cowpunk. Mama raised us on country, and I thought the combination of country and punk was cool."

"And you had the right attitude to pull it off, with how rebellious you were." I thought about the troubled kid I used to be. "In the beginning, I did everything my aunt and uncle told me to do. But later, I copped plenty of attitude, too."

"Yes, of course, you pounding away on the piano."

"I still play that way when I'm all alone, letting my frustrations out."

She softly asked, "Did you cry when your mom died?"

"I bawled like a baby. But that's the last time I cried. What about you?"

"I cried when my mama passed. But I've cried a lot since then. Not just when I'm sad, but when I'm mad, too."

"You never cried around me." I'd never seen that side of her. "But we barely knew each other."

"We're making up for that now."

That was for damned sure. I'd never shared my feelings with a woman before. But maybe it was part of being sober, of learning how to be someone's lover without being wasted. I was different now. Alice was, too, with her thirst for a husband.

I popped off with a smile, teasing her, poking at her hair again. "I'm surprised 'White Wedding' isn't your karaoke song."

She kicked me under the sheet. "That's not funny. Have you seen how goth that old video is? The nails in the coffin and all that."

"Says the girl who already knows what kind of engagement ring she wants. A black diamond. That actually sounds kind of goth."

She snorted. "Maybe you should write a song about it."

"Maybe I will." I'd already decided that she could be my muse. "Alice in Spencerland. Who wouldn't want to write about you?"

"It'd better be a good song."

"It'll be my best." Or I hoped it would. But I couldn't just rush something out. It had to come naturally. "Do you want to watch TV?" I asked. "As long as we're lying around, we might as well stream something."

"That sounds nice. But I'm going to put my bra and panties back on first."

"That's fine." I'd already climbed into my boxers earlier. I watched her get out of bed and slip into her underwear.

"What should we watch?" she asked, returning to my side and propping up a pillow for herself.

"I don't know. Let's look and see what our choices are."

After scrolling through tons of movies and shows, we picked *Sons of Anarchy*, even though we'd both seen the entire series before.

"This is one of my favorite shows," she said.

"Mine, too. It's pretty twisted, though."

"That's why I like it."

"Same here." Which made us twisted people, I supposed. But that was part of why we'd hooked up to begin with. Alice and I weren't normal. We'd had problems from the start.

Turning silent, we binged on the show.

We watched the first three episodes of the first season, before she decided it was time to go. By now, it was long past dusk. We'd spent the entire day together.

I offered her a sweatshirt to cover her torn blouse. She accepted it, and I got the feeling she liked wearing my clothes. I wondered when I was going to see her again. Last time, we just texted each other when we wanted sex. But this time, we hadn't discussed the specifics.

We hadn't talked about working together again, either. Maybe I would benefit from having her as my regular stylist. Then again, did I even need a regular stylist? It wasn't as if I was attending fancy events or doing photo shoots every day. Mostly, I was just a songwriter, working from home.

While she finished getting dressed, I mentioned my upcoming trip. "Did I tell you that I was going to Los Angeles next week?"

"No, you didn't. Is it for business?"

I nodded. "I'll be meeting with the music director of a film who wants me to compose the score."

She cocked her head. "How long will you be gone?"

"About three days. I reserved a bungalow at the Chateau Marmont." I shrugged, smiled a little. "I chartered a private plane, too." I forged ahead with the invitation. "You should come with me."

"Really?" She sounded surprised. "Are you sure I won't be in the way?"

"I'm positive." It would solve the issue of when I was going to see her again. "It would be nice to have the company and since we agreed to keep hanging out for a while, I figured why not travel together."

She furrowed her brow. "We didn't agree to hang out, Spencer. We agreed to keep sleeping together."

"I know." I hesitated, hoping I wasn't biting off more than I could chew by whisking her off on a trip. "But it's just for fun." I wasn't suggesting anything more. "Besides, have you ever been to LA?"

"Yes, but I spent all of my time in the fashion district. I've never really seen the sights." She paused, as if she was debating the fun we were supposed to have. "If I go with you, will you give me a tour?" she asked.

"Absolutely." I moved closer to where she stood. "I'll rent a fast car and take you wherever you want to go."

"Now how can I say no to that?" She smiled, the idea of traveling with me obviously growing on her. "I like fast cars."

"What about fast men?" As quick as could be, I kissed her, cementing our deal. But I didn't tell her that this would be the first time that I would be returning to LA since I'd left home. I would tackle that anxiety later. For now, I just wanted to kiss her a few more times.

After Alice left, I got the dogs from the rescue and brought them home. They crawled straight into their beds and slept. My cell phone rang, and I checked the screen. It was Kirby.

"Hey," I answered. "What's up?"

"I was wondering if I could come by and talk to you," he replied.

"Today?" I glanced at my piano. I planned on working for the rest of the evening, keeping myself from obsessing about the LA trip. I was glad that Alice would be joining me, but I was still nervous about returning to the place where I'd been immersed in so much pain.

"Is this a bad time for you?" He sounded upset.

"No, it's fine." I couldn't turn him away, not after everything he'd done for me. "Are you okay?"

"I'll explain when I get there. I'm in my car, so it won't be long."

"All right. I'll see you soon." I hoped he wasn't having the urge to drink or use. He'd been clean and sober for a lot longer than me. He was my rock, the person I relied on. If he faltered, was I strong enough to get him through it?

He arrived looking like he was headed to a funeral, shrouded in black, but without his usual silver jewelry or Western bling. We went into my living room, and he plopped onto a chair. His leg was jittery.

"Did somebody die?" I asked.

"Yeah, me," he said.

I asked the next question, dreading his response. "What happened? Did you get high? Did you drink?"

He scowled at me. "No."

I sighed in relief. But he was still scowling. I

watched him run his hand across his beard. I'd never seen him so agitated.

"Did you have a fight with one of your kids?" I was playing twenty questions, trying to drag it out of him. He'd come over to tell me his problem, but now he seemed reluctant to say it.

He blew out a windy breath. "Everything is fine with my sons."

"Your lady then?" Kirby was dating a woman who worked for the Country Music Hall of Fame. In the past, he hadn't been faithful to anyone. But as far as I knew, he was loyal to her.

"Debra is fine, too." He snared my gaze. "This is about Alice."

My heart knocked against my rib cage. Did he suspect that I was involved with her? Had he figured it out?

Did it matter if he did? I asked myself. She and I were both consenting adults. It wasn't Kirby's place to reprimand me. I could sleep with whoever I wanted.

"I lied to you," he said.

My pulse jumped. "About Alice?"

"And her mom." He scooted forward in the leather chair he was occupying. "I knew Cathy before Alice was ever born. About nine months before," he added.

Holy crap, I thought.

He got up and went over to the bar, pouring himself a soda. I watched him, making sure that he didn't spike it.

"Is Alice your daughter?" I asked, point-blank.

He winced. "I can't say for sure, but there's a darned good possibility."

"Why in the hell didn't you tell me this before?"

"Because you caught me off guard last time, and I panicked. I haven't told anyone else, but no one has suspected it except for you."

I considered how this news was going to impact Alice. Would she explode in a devastating rage? Would she sink to the floor and cry? Would she come after Kirby with a knife? I imagined all sorts of horrible reactions.

I tried to clear those awful things from my mind but I couldn't shake them completely. "How long have you known that she might be yours?"

He returned to his chair. "I suspected it when I met Alice for the first time."

I gaped at him. "She was only nineteen then." They'd met for the first time in his son's law office, when they'd negotiated the terms of the settlement related to her mom's songs and signed the papers. "I can't believe you suspected it all this time."

"I wasn't sure. I mean, it was just a feeling I had. But I couldn't remember exactly when I was with Cathy. As stoned as I used to be, I wasn't keeping track of who and when." He gulped his soda. "But then, a few months ago, I was going through some old stuff I had in storage, and I came across a letter that Cathy had written to me during our first affair. When I saw the date on it, I realized that the timeline could absolutely make me Alice's dad."

I studied him from where I stood. "So, let me get

this straight. You had two affairs with Cathy? The first one when Alice might've been conceived, and then another one years later?"

"Yes, but Cathy approached me the second time with the sole purpose of trying to sell her songs. She was struggling to raise her daughters and was hoping to make a better life for them. She hadn't intended to sleep with me again, but I lured her back into bed without buying the songs."

"And she never told you that Alice might be yours?"

"No. She didn't say a word about that. She kept contacting me about the songs. But she didn't mention Alice."

"Don't you find that odd? If she was struggling to raise her kids, then why didn't she request a paternity test and try to get child support from you? You're a rich man. The payout could have been substantial."

"I know, but maybe she didn't want to stir up something that would make her look bad in her children's eyes. Maybe she couldn't bear to admit that she'd cheated on Joel when she was with me the first time or that her daughters might have two different fathers."

"That could be it. But are you sure the timeline of that letter is accurate? You could be confused about being Alice's dad."

"I'm not confused. I even told Alice during our first meeting that if I ever had a daughter, I'd want it to be someone like her. There was just something about her that made me feel as if she could be mine, and now I know that I wasn't so far off the mark."

I wasn't going to dispute his emotions or the paternal feelings he had for her. I appreciated that his heart was in the right place, but there was still going to be hell to pay with Alice. "When are you going to tell her? As difficult as it's going to be, she has a right to know."

"I was hoping that you could help me get closer to her before I say anything."

"Me?" I flinched. "That's not a good idea."

He shot me a chastising look. "Why? Because you used to get drunk and sleep with her? I'm not an idiot, Spencer. There's no way that you and Alice had a respectful thing going. With as wild as both of you used to be, that's just not feasible."

"You suspected all along that I was lying?"

"Yes, I did. But I lied to you, too, so I think that makes us even."

"I'm seeing her again." As long as we were clearing the air, I laid that out there, too. "But Alice and I agreed that it's only a temporary thing. She wants a husband someday, and I couldn't even begin to contemplate a relationship." My only goal was to stay sober, but I figured that went without saying, especially to Kirby.

"I understand. But promise me that you'll be good to her while you're together."

"I will." The last thing I wanted was to hurt her. "She's going to LA with me next week. I have some business dealings there, and I invited her to come along."

His gaze sought mine. "Will you help me get closer to her?"

As desperate as he was, how could I refuse him? He'd never turned me down for anything before. "I'll certainly try. But I have no idea how I'm supposed to accomplish it."

"Just say nice things about me."

"She gets mad when I do that. But I'll keep doing it and try to bring her around." It was obvious how much Kirby wanted to be her father. That in his heart, he already loved her. "I don't want her to keep hating you."

He rewarded me with a smile. "I think you'll be a positive influence on her. If anyone can make her see the good in me, it's you."

I hoped he wasn't giving me more credit than I deserved. "I'll do my best. But how long are we going to keep this a secret?"

"I'll tell her as soon as you think she's ready."

"Then we'll just take it day by day." I didn't expect overnight results, if I got them at all. But I wanted to make a difference. No one had ever needed me for something so important.

And regardless of how it turned out, the possibility of Kirby being Alice's father was about as important as it got.

Eight

Alice

I sat on Tracy's sofa, surrounded by her woodsy décor, clutching an embroidered pillow to my chest—one of those old-fashioned "Home Sweet Home" things. The scented candle she'd burned earlier had gone out, smoldering down to its wick, as I told her about sleeping with Spencer.

"The sex was amazing. And so was the time we spent together afterward." I couldn't deny how attentive Spencer had become.

She set her chair in motion, an old bentwood rocker she'd gotten at a flea market. "Then why do you still seem scared?"

"It's my fear of getting too close. While I was with

him, I kept warning myself not to get attached, but what if I do?"

"You're bound to feel that way after so many years of being alone. But the idea is to have some fun, right? Isn't that why he invited you to go to LA with him?"

"Yes, but our affair isn't going to last. He already told me that he can't be my Mr. Right."

"Is that what you want him to be?"

"I don't know. I'm just confused, I guess."

"Then maybe you shouldn't go to LA with him."

"But I want to see him again." I wanted to crawl back into his big strong arms.

She watched me squeeze the pillow. "Then you have to decide what's best for you."

"Truthfully, I just want to have some fun and quit worrying about it. But my past keeps coming back to haunt me. The wild girl who'd made all of the wrong decisions."

"You're not that girl anymore, Al. You've grown up since then. And in my opinion, you're allowed to have some adult fun, to be with a sexy guy, even if he's not Mr. Right."

I nodded, grateful that she was encouraging me to live a little. "After five years of celibacy, I deserve to have a good time." To quit beating myself up about the past, I thought, and to quit panicking about getting attached. "I'll just have a great affair with Spencer. Then later, I'll find the man I'm meant to be with." Somehow, someway, I would meet the guy of my dreams—when all of this was over with Spencer.

She smiled. "There you go. Your decision is made."

But would it be that easy? I asked myself. God, I hoped so. Nothing about my life had been easy this far.

Tracy went silent, and I got the sneaking suspicion that she was thinking about her ex. I watched her, waiting to see if she would mention him.

Then she said, "Not that it should matter, but I wonder how well Spencer knows Dash. If they're friends or just new acquaintances."

Bingo, I thought. She couldn't go a week without Dash's name coming up. Deep down, she was as troubled as I was. "I don't know. But I can ask him, if you want."

"Sure, okay." She seemed reflective, as always, when it came to her ex. "Do you think Spencer knows that Dash and I used to be engaged?"

"I have no idea. But I can ask him that, too."

"A lot of people in this town know. But a lot don't. I guess it depends on how gossipy they are."

"Spencer doesn't seem particularly gossipy. But he has been talking about himself and his family, telling me about his past. He never used to do that before."

"It's good that he's opening up. That he trusts you with his past."

"It's been nice having real conversations with him. I think there are still some subjects that make him uncomfortable, though."

"Dash had trouble sharing his feelings with me. And when he did share them, they weren't very comforting."

Because Dash didn't believe in love, I thought, and Tracy did. "They say love hurts."

She touched a hand to her stomach. Was she thinking about the baby she'd miscarried? The child she should've had with Dash?

She looked up at me. "It only hurts when it doesn't work the way it's supposed to. But it's going to be perfect when it happens to you. You're going to marry someone who's going to love you to the ends of the earth."

"Someone who isn't Spencer," I said, confirming that no matter how wonderful my affair with him was, it had absolutely nothing to do with love. I couldn't risk my heart on a man who wasn't interested in marriage.

On the night before Spencer and I were scheduled to leave for Los Angeles, my sister asked me for an emergency favor. Her nanny was sick, and she needed someone to babysit the twins. Naturally, I agreed to watch them. I adored Hudson and Hailey.

I was in the master bedroom with Mary, and so were the kids. They loved watching their mommy get fixed up. She and Brandon were attending a black-tie event, something they often did. Brandon was downstairs, attired in his tux and waiting for his wife. He'd greeted me earlier, when I'd first come to the door. He was a wonderful husband and father, even if he was Kirby's son.

I turned my attention to the kids. They sat on their parents' bed, dressed in their pajamas. At four years old, they were smart and spry, with their dark auburn hair and bright blue eyes. Hailey was being a pistol, as usual. Since I'd arrived, she'd already spilled some of Mommy's perfume on the floor. Hudson hadn't done anything, except smile at me like the pint-sized gentleman that he was.

"What do you think?" Mary asked, as she spun around in her emerald-green gown.

"Mommy pretty," Hudson said.

"Very pretty," I agreed. I was Mary's stylist, so I'd picked out the dress for her. Her closet was filled with choices I'd made. "Your hair looks amazing, too." She'd styled her long red locks in a chic updo. When we were younger, she'd always looked like the girl-next-door type. These days, she was far more glamorous.

"What about you?" Mary asked her daughter. "Do you think I need some earrings? Maybe a necklace?"

"Yes!" Hailey bounded off the bed.

She always chose the jewelry her mother wore on formal occasions. But the kid had a great eye. She'd inherited her style from me. Her rebellion, too, I supposed. Even Spencer had teased me about that, and he didn't even know Hailey.

I watched my niece sort through her mother's jewels. She examined each piece carefully. Of course, Mary didn't leave it around for Hailey to get into on her own. She kept it locked in a safe. Otherwise the little girl might be tempted to wear it herself or put it on her dolls or bury it in the yard like a hidden treasure.

Hailey chose a diamond ensemble with ruby accents that complemented the shiny red soles on Mary's heels.

"Now Mommy perfect," she said.

"Yes, she is." My sister had everything I hoped for:

a kind and loving husband, two beautiful children, a successful career.

"Will you tell Daddy that I'm almost ready?" Mary said to the kids.

"Yup!" Hailey pulled her brother down off the bed, and they dashed off, excited to deliver the message.

"What's going on?" Mary asked me after the twins were gone. "You seem preoccupied."

Rather than hide my feelings completely, I said, "I'm seeing someone. In fact, I'm taking a trip with him. We're leaving tomorrow afternoon. He has business in LA, and he asked me to accompany him."

"Really? Who is he?"

"His name is Spencer Riggs."

"The songwriter?" She angled her head. "He's friends with Kirby, isn't he?"

"Yes. Kirby recommended me to him. But I knew Spencer from a long time ago, too."

"Is it serious?"

"No." I wasn't about to admit that he was the last guy I'd slept with before I became celibate. Mary didn't know about my sordid history with Spencer, and I wasn't keen on telling her, either. "He's just someone I'm seeing for now."

"Are you still hoping to meet the right man someday?"

"Yes, I am. I just have to be patient enough to find him."

She glanced at her wedding ring. "I hope falling in love is easier for you than it was for me. The way I lied to Brandon in the beginning, hiding my identity from him."

"I still feel awful for being such a big part of that." I'd orchestrated her deception, encouraging her to hurt Brandon. I'd believed at the time that he'd been involved in destroying Mama, which wasn't true, and Mary had gotten close to him under false pretenses to find out the truth.

"It's over now." She gazed at her ring again. "Everything turned out the way it should."

I swallowed the lump in my throat, envious of her life, but glad for her, too. "You better get going or you'll be late." I picked up her gold clutch and handed it to her.

She took the purse, checking her belongings inside of it. "Brandon must be keeping the kids busy. Otherwise they would be back to see what's taking me so long."

We went downstairs together. Me in my comfy babysitting outfit, and Mary in her gown.

Brandon was in his home office, sitting at the computer desk with the twins on his lap. He was letting them type on his laptop. Brandon was an entertainment lawyer, a high-society guy who loved art and music and fine wine. He had smooth black hair, regal features and stunning blue eyes, like the kids.

"I'm ready," Mary said from behind them.

Brandon spun around on his chair, taking Hailey and Hudson for a spin, too. He let out a low whistle and said, "There's my gorgeous wife."

She smiled. "And there's my handsome husband."

The twins jumped off his lap and ran over to me. They seemed to know that their daddy was going to stand up and kiss their mommy. Sure enough, he did. It was just a chaste kiss, but it made my heart jump, reminding me of the future I longed to have.

But in the interim, I had Spencer to keep me entertained. And tomorrow, I would be headed to California with him, immersed in lust and passion.

Spencer picked me up at my condo and loaded my bags into his truck. I'd overpacked, but I was a clotheshorse, so that was normal for me.

As he pulled out of the parking lot, I said, "You look like a California boy today." He wore his usual torn jeans, a plain T-shirt and slip-on sneakers with a checkerboard pattern.

"I just wanted to be comfortable." He frowned. "I probably should have mentioned this before, but I haven't been back since I left."

"This is your first time going home?" I considered the circumstances. "I haven't been back to Oklahoma since I left, either." I was settled in Nashville now, and there didn't seem to be any reason to return to where I'd been raised.

He drove toward the interstate that would take us to the airport. "I have good and bad memories of living in LA. But the bad ones always seem to take over."

"What's your favorite part about LA?" I asked, trying to cheer him up. I knew the pitfalls of being consumed with the bad stuff.

"The beaches," he replied, his mood brightening already. "I used to surf a little."

"I can see you doing that." Tall and tan, with his

skin tasting like saltwater. I touched a finger to my lips, almost as if I could taste it on him, too. It made me want to kiss him, everywhere, all over his body.

"Venice Beach was one of my teenage hangouts. I liked the artsy vibe, the weirdness, I guess. The surfing was good, too."

I was getting more excited about this trip, anxious to spend time with him. "Can we go there?"

"Sure. I think you'd enjoy it."

"I wonder if three days will be enough to fit everything in." Suddenly, it seemed too short, too rushed.

He changed lanes, then glanced over at me. "Do you want to stay for a few extra days?"

"Do you think we could?" I'd already made up my mind to have a good time and try not to stress about the future. But somehow, I still had butterflies in my stomach over it.

"I don't see why not. I can check with the hotel about extending the reservation."

"Then let's do it." The longer we stayed, the more fun we could have—in and out of bed.

Or at least until my butterflies subsided. Or our affair ended. Whichever came first.

This was the life, I thought, as we boarded the plane. We checked in easily, with comfort and style, using a different part of the airport from where the commercial flights took off and landed. Both the pilot and our flight attendant greeted us, introducing themselves and giving us special treatment.

Once we were settled into our seats, I said to Spencer, "I've never flown this way before."

He studied me, his dark eyes locking onto mine. "You've never been on a private plane?"

"No, never." Aside from my association with Mary and Brandon, I wasn't part of an elite crowd.

"My aunt and uncle used to charter planes. It spoiled me, I suppose. As much I hated living with them, I appreciated some of the luxuries."

"Who wouldn't?" This jet had a glitzy black-and-tan décor with a dining table, two sets of sofas and a big-screen TV. "I used to rent party boats on the river. I burned through a lot of my settlement money, trying to live the high life and show off to my friends. But it caught up with me. I only took the job with you because I wanted to work with Derek and I was worried about my finances."

"I figured it was something like that." He nudged my arm, his elbow purposely bumping mine. "I guess it's a good thing I didn't fire you."

"Smart aleck." I adjusted my seat belt to fit more securely.

He watched me. "You're not a nervous flyer, are you?"

"Maybe a little." Soon we would be taxiing down the runway. "I've never really flown that much."

"You can have a glass of wine, if that will help. Or a cocktail or whatever you prefer. I don't expect people to avoid drinking around me."

"That's okay. I don't need anything." I wasn't comfortable putting alcohol under his nose, in spite of his claim not to care. I chanced to ask, "Is it tough staying sober?"

He sat perfectly still, almost as if he didn't want to react. Then he said, "I already told you that I can resist the temptation. Otherwise, I wouldn't have a bar at my house."

"Sometimes you still seem restless, like you used to be."

As the plane started to move, he replied, "You seem that way, too."

"Yes, but I'm not a recovering alcoholic." To me, that made my restlessness less dangerous than his.

"Don't worry about it, okay? Kirby will always be there to help if I need it." He watched me again, deeply, closely. "One way or another, I'm going to make you see him for the decent guy that he is."

"That's never going to happen," I shot back.

"You're always so damned stubborn." His voice turned rough, sexy, commanding. "Maybe I'll just have to kiss you to keep you in line."

My body went unbearably warm. The plane was gaining speed, making my breath catch in my throat. "Right now?"

"Hell, yes." He leaned over and slanted his mouth over mine, using his tongue to tempt me.

I closed my eyes and returned his kiss, needing him, wanting him. In the background, I could hear the rumble of the engine. I jolted as the plane bounded into the air.

But mostly, it was my lover jarring my emotions and lifting me straight off the ground.

Nine

Spencer

The Chateau Marmont had been inspired by a Gothic French chateau, and the bungalow I'd rented was artfully crafted, offering a breezy sitting area, an elegant bedroom and bath, a private patio and a fully stocked kitchen. I'd requested groceries ahead of time, giving us the option of dining in or going out, depending on our mood.

Alice seemed impressed. She wandered in and out of the rooms, with a girlish light in her eyes.

After we entered the bedroom, she removed her sandals and flopped back on the ornately carved bed, her sundress billowing around her. I wanted to free my mind and simply enjoy looking at her, but my thoughts were too damned scattered.

Was Kirby her father? I wondered.

There was no way to know for sure, not without a paternity test. Kirby seemed certain of it, making me inclined to believe it, as well. Yet, if Alice was his daughter, I was still baffled about why Cathy had kept quiet about it. I hadn't considered this before, but maybe Kirby himself had been the problem. Maybe Cathy had concerns about his addictions back then and didn't want him participating in Alice's life. Whatever her reasons, things were different now. Alice was a grown woman, and Kirby was clean and sober. If Cathy were alive today, she wouldn't have anything to worry about.

"What made you choose this hotel?" Alice asked, pulling me back into our surroundings.

"The music director I'll be meeting with lives nearby, so I figured it would be a convenient location." I glanced toward the window. Sunshine slashed through the blinds, creating a mysterious pattern on the floor. "I was fascinated by the things I'd heard about it, too. In the old Hollywood days, they used to say that this was the place to go to get into trouble. It has a history of celebrities behaving badly here."

"Really?" She sat up and leaned against the headboard. "Oh, how fun."

"Yes, but the really wild stuff was kept secret. All of the rooms, bungalows and cottages are soundproof, and the staff has always been discreet, particularly during that era. The Chateau was considered a luxurious hideout back then." I almost felt as if Alice and I were hiding out. Former lovers renewing their affair. That, in itself, seemed sort of scandalous.

"Can't you just imagine what old Hollywood must have been like?" She struck a glamorous pose, as if she was tossing a long, sleek scarf over her shoulder.

"Yeah, I can imagine it." I could actually see her dressed like a movie star. "But tragic things occurred here, too, later on. John Belushi overdosed in one of the bungalows." I figured she would know who he was, given her interest in the '70s and '80s.

"Do you know which bungalow it was?" she asked.

"I think it's over that way." I'd already looked it up on the net. "I'm sure they've remodeled it since then, but there have been reports of him haunting it over the years. I don't know if that's true or just people making up stories."

Her gaze sought mine. "Do you believe in ghosts?"

"I'd like to think that they're real. When I was a teenager, I used to go to our old apartment and park in front of the building, wishing my mom would appear. She never did, though."

She gave me a sympathetic look. "Was it hard for you when you left LA? Did you feel as if you were leaving her behind?"

I nodded, my heart clenching at the memory. "She loved this town. But it changed for me after she died."

"Will you take me to see your old apartment? We can park out front the way you used to do."

"Maybe we can do that tonight." She understood my loss. Her mother was gone, too. But how was she going to feel when she learned that Kirby might be her dad?

She got to her feet and came over to me. I put my arms around her, stroking a hand down her back and inhaling the citrusy scent of her perfume.

Now that her paternity was on the line, should I work toward discovering mine, too?

We separated, and I said, "I'm going to look for my dad. Once we get back to Nashville, I'll submit my DNA to the ancestry websites and see where it leads. There are two main sites I'm going to use."

"That's wonderful. I think it's important for you to know where you came from and who your father is."

"It's worth a try." Was my old man out there somewhere? Would I find him? "But I'm not going to idealize him like I did when I was a kid."

"Are you still concerned that he might reject you?"

"Yes." In her case, Kirby wanted to be her dad. She was lucky in that way, even if she didn't know it yet.

She comforted me, skimming her fingers along my jaw. "Just try to be positive."

I embraced her again. "You're right. I need to believe it's possible." Because who could say what would happen for sure? Maybe I would get lucky and my father would be as interested in me as Kirby was in her.

In the evening, after Alice and I dined at a new steak house in Studio City, I drove the Porsche Cayman I'd rented to my old apartment. It wasn't the best neighborhood, but it wasn't the worst, either. Mostly it catered to striving actors, models and musicians. Some regular folks, too. Not everyone had stars in their eyes. Some of the surrounding areas were laced with drug activity, but I'd always steered clear of those parts. I'd never been a druggie, not like Kirby and some of the other addicts I knew. For that much, I was grateful. I didn't need any more demons.

I parallel parked, wedging the car into a tight space, with a streetlamp overhead giving us a bit of light.

Alice sat in the passenger seat in a slim black outfit and designer heels. She'd changed out of the sundress and into something sexier.

And now here we were, where I used to live. It looked the same to me. The Spanish-style accents: the tile roof, the stucco exterior, the arches. There wasn't a lot of foliage, just a few low hedges on either side.

"Which unit was yours?" she asked.

I pointed to a second-story window. "That was my bedroom. I used to keep some of my toy soldiers on the windowsill, lined up and ready for war."

"I wonder who lives there now."

"I have no idea." The blinds were closed. "When it was my room, it had blackout curtains. I thought those were cool. Mom decorated her room with a seashell motif. She was even buried at sea."

Alice turned to face me. "Did you sprinkle the ashes?"

"My aunt didn't think it was appropriate for a child my age. She had the captain of the boat do it."

Sorrow edged her voice. "That wasn't fair to you."

"Nothing ever really was. But later when I started surfing, I felt at peace in the ocean. Sometimes I would run my hands through the water and imagine that Mom was there, all around me."

"I know what you mean. My mother was cremated, too. Mary and I sprinkled her ashes at a park she used to take us to when we were kids, and that's where I'll always think of her."

"I wish I could have met your mom." I didn't know much about her, other than what Alice or Kirby had told me. But I was beginning to feel a kinship toward her. "We could've shared our experiences about songwriting."

"I think she would have liked that." She glanced out the windshield. "But now I'm getting emotional, sitting here on your childhood street, talking about life and death."

I felt it, too. But I didn't want to admit how deeply this moment was affecting me. "You suggested coming here."

"I know. But normally the only other person I ever have these types of conversations with is Tracy." She hesitated, squinting at me. "Did you know that she used to be engaged to Dash Smith?"

I frowned a little. "No, but is there a reason I should be aware of that?"

"Not necessarily. Except that you're going to be working with Dash on his next album, aren't you?"

"We haven't collaborated on any songs yet. But we plan to once he gets off tour."

"How well do you know him?"

"Not well. We've only met a couple of times."

"He's been asking Tracy to do a duet, but she isn't interested in making a record with him."

That was news to me, but all of this was. "If she changes her mind, then maybe I'll be working with her, too."

"I don't think she's going to change her mind."

I didn't ask what the problem was or why their engagement ended, but I did say, "Just so you know, Kirby figured us out."

She flinched. "What?"

"He could tell that I was lying about my past with you."

She set her mouth in a grim line. "Did you tell him that we were together now?"

"Yes, but I explained that it was only temporary."

"And what was his reaction?"

"He made me promise to be good to you."

She scoffed. "As if he cares."

"He does care." I couldn't tell her how much. She wasn't anywhere near being ready to hear the truth. But at least I was planting whatever seeds were possible.

She huffed, headstrong as ever. "It's none of Kirby's business what we do."

"Yeah, but it's still nice of him to be looking out for your best interests. Speaking of which, do you think we should just be open with everyone else, too?"

"I already told Tracy that I slept with you again."

I should have suspected as much. "Does your sister know?"

"She knows I took this trip with you."

"Then it doesn't matter if people see us together in Nashville, does it?"

She scrutinized me, looking me up and down. "I

guess we could be open about it. That's probably better than keeping it a secret, like we did in the past."

"Gee, thanks for the enthusiasm." I leaned over and gave her a rough kiss, refusing to let her get the best of me.

I almost expected her to push me away, but she climbed over the console and onto my lap. Was she trying to prove that she was the boss?

She straddled me in my seat, rocking back and forth, a triumphant expression on her face. I wanted to reach around to fondle her ass, but I kept my arms at my sides, refusing to let her win. She rubbed me some more, bumping my fly, causing friction.

Electricity. Human sparks.

Was she proposing a quickie in the car? Was that her intention? I groaned and said, "We can't do this here. If we get caught, we'll get busted for indecent exposure."

She shrugged. "I'm not exposing anything, are you?"

I glanced down the front of her blouse and spied her bra, the push-up kind that created extra cleavage. "You're torturing me."

"That's the idea." She returned to her own seat, leaving me with a raging hard-on. She knew how to make me suffer.

But I knew how to seduce her, too.

"This isn't over," I said, letting her know that I was going to do unspeakable things to her.

As soon as we got back to the hotel.

After a night of rowdy sex, I awakened before Alice. I leaned on my elbow and watched her sleep.

She looked innocent, with no makeup and wispy hair. Her spiky do was flat this morning.

What was going to happen when our affair was over? Would I become abstinent again? Or would I take another lover? Replacing her was going to be difficult. I hated to even think about it.

I crept out of bed and climbed into my jeans. Alice stirred, turning sideways in her sleep. We'd left the windows open, and now a breeze was dancing around the room.

I stood back and leaned against a wall, wondering if she was dreaming. If she was, I hoped her dreams were soft and safe.

I used to have recurring nightmares of monsters clawing at me, chasing me inside my aunt and uncle's mansion. Sometimes I still had them, except the monsters attacked my sobriety now, taunting me to fail, to take another drink, to destroy the man I was working so hard to become.

Alice stirred again, coming awake. She reached over to my side of the bed and found it empty. Had she been hoping to cuddle?

She sat up, and the sheet fell to her waist, giving me a delicious view of her breasts. She glanced toward the wall, where I was, and gasped.

"Oh, my God, Spencer. You scared me."

"Sorry."

"What an image to wake up to." She blinked as if I was a tall, dark mirage, coming to life from the desert air. "My heart is still pounding."

"I'm going to make a pot of coffee."

She adjusted the sheet, pulling it back up and over her breasts. "Should I meet you in the kitchen?"

"Why don't you stay here, and I'll bring you a cup."

She ran her hand through her hair, letting it flutter through her fingers. "Are you going to make breakfast, too?"

"I can whip up some eggs." I quirked a deliberate smile. "Unless you want frozen pizza."

She grinned. "Nice try. But I'll take the eggs."

I left her alone and went into the kitchen. I'd never actually cooked for anyone before, at least not from scratch. But I could handle breakfast.

I brewed the coffee, fried four strips of bacon and scrambled three eggs. I made toast, too, and buttered it. I looked around for a spot of color and went onto the patio, plucking a purple-and-yellow bloom from one of the pots.

I prepared a tray, placing the flower beside her plate. I included milk and sugar for her coffee. I preferred mine black.

I returned to the bedroom, set the tray in front of her and removed my cup.

She glanced up at me. She was dressed now. While I was in the kitchen, she'd borrowed one of my T-shirts. For all I knew, she was wearing a pair of my boxers, too. I couldn't see her lower half, but I rather hoped that she was. Her interest in wearing my clothes turned me on.

"Thank you. This looks great," she said. "But why aren't you eating?"

"I'm not hungry. Besides, I've got my business meeting today, and it's supposed to be a brunch."

She added a dollop of milk and two packets of sugar to her coffee. "I'll probably take an Uber to Rodeo Drive while you're gone. It's on my list of places to see."

I sat at a nearby desk and pushed the hotel stationery out of my way. "There's some nice stores on Sunset, too." I made a deadpan expression. "You could check out Hustler Hollywood."

She rolled her eyes. "The erotica boutique? I think I'll pass." She hesitated, seeming a bit more serious. "Unless you want me to go there."

"It's totally up to you, but I was only kidding around."

A few breathless beats later, she said, "I think I better stick to regular stores."

I sipped my coffee, amused by her newfound sense of propriety. "Yeah, after all of the raunchy stuff we did last night, who needs sex toys, anyway."

She threw the flower at me. But it flopped onto the floor, missing me by a mile.

I came up with a legitimate plan. "You know what we should do? Take some vacation selfies together and post them online."

"I guess that would be all right. But let's not go overboard with kissing pictures or anything like that. I don't want to seem unprofessional."

"Actually, I think it'll boost your profile to be romantically linked to me. Not to brag, but I have lots of followers."

"I know how popular you are." She gazed at me from beneath her lashes. "And I suppose you're right. Your followers will probably take an interest in me. A positive one, I hope." She bit into her toast. After she ate half of it, she added, "We didn't take selfies with each other before."

"No, but remember how we used to sext?" My cup clanked when I put it down. "And the nude pictures you sent me?"

Her cheeks went pink, an uncharacteristic blush for such a naughty girl. I didn't call her on it. I kept the visual to myself, wanting to remember it later.

"You sent some to me, too," she said.

"Mine were dick pics. Any idiot can do those. The stuff you did was beautiful." Alluring, sensual, sweetly wicked. I wished I'd saved them, tucked them away in a secret file. "Will you send me one later today?"

Her jaw dropped. "While you're at your meeting? I wouldn't dare."

I challenged her, flirting, playing a lover's game. "Then at least come over here and kiss me."

She set the tray aside, baiting me right back. "I think you should come over here."

She didn't have to ask me twice. I leaped onto the bed and tackled her, making her laugh and squeal. I lowered the sheet. She wasn't wearing my boxers. She didn't have any bottoms on at all.

I grabbed my phone off the nightstand and snapped a picture of her butt. She tried to wrestle the device away from me, and I took another one. I knew she would make me delete them, but for now, I was having fun.

I liked the feeling, the freedom. At times like this, I wanted to pretend that my life was easy. But there was nothing easy about what I'd been through. Alice's past wasn't easy, either. But at the moment, we were together—and enjoying every playful second of it.

Ten

Alice

Spencer and I sat side by side on a bench, sipping blueberry slushies. As we looked out at the ocean, dusk dimmed the sky.

We'd spent the entire day here at Venice Beach, soaking up the sun, gathering seashells, swimming in the ocean and eating junk food. Spencer had also bought me some trinkets, including a temporary tattoo, but I hadn't applied it yet.

"It's probably raining again in Nashville," I said. "I can't believe how nice it is here." Even now, with the sun setting over the water, it was comfortably warm.

"We got lucky with the weather. Sometimes it's

chilly in the spring. But I like the beach when it's cold, too."

I glanced around. There were still people everywhere, treating it like a summer day. Or evening, now that daylight was waning. "I'll bet it has a completely different energy when it's cold."

He nodded. "It's calmer, quieter. A good place to be alone and reflect."

"Did you used to do that a lot? Come here to be alone?"

"Yeah." He turned to look at me. "I'm glad I'm not alone right now."

"So am I." My heart skipped a beat. "I could get used to this. To the beach," I clarified. I could get used to being with him, too. A part of me never wanted our time together to end. But that wasn't something I should be imagining, not when I knew that our affair wasn't meant to last.

He set his drink down. "Let's put your new tattoo on."

"We'll need a damp cloth. It won't stick without water."

"We can use a corner of a towel." He removed one from our beach bag. "I'll be right back."

I watched him walk over to a drinking fountain across the boardwalk. While he was gone, I dug through my shopping bag for the tattoo, a design with black roses and a swirly pink butterfly. Spencer had picked it out for me.

He returned with the damp towel and resumed his seat. He looked natural in the setting, tall and tan in a ribbed tank top and colorful board shorts. Me? I'd slathered on a high SPF lotion to keep from getting burned.

"Where should we put it?" he asked. "Where do you want it?"

"Where do you think it should go?" He knew my body well, and I trusted him to make the decision.

"How about at your bikini line? Then I can see it every time I touch you there."

Please, yes. I got up and removed my sarong, standing before him in my bathing suit, tingling with anticipation.

No one paid us any mind, not even when he tugged my bikini bottoms down a little. Immersed in his task, he saturated the tattoo with moisture from the corner of the towel, holding it against my skin.

Sixty second later, he peeled off the paper and exposed my new body art. In the silence that followed, he dabbed off the excess water and rubbed a tiny bit of sunscreen on it.

He righted my bikini bottoms. "The lotion will help make it last longer."

I glanced down at the design. It was partially concealed beneath my bathing suit, but still beautiful. It would look even better when I was naked in his arms.

I reached for my sarong, covering myself up. He watched me with unfettered desire in his eyes.

We went back to drinking our slushies. I needed to cool off. He obviously did, too.

After we finished them, he said, "Your lips are blue."

"So are yours."

We laughed and took a selfie. We'd taken tons of them today, posting them on Instagram. Our affair was definitely out in the open.

"Do you think we'll remain friends after we stop seeing each other?" I asked, battling a sudden burst of emotion.

"I don't know. What do you think?"

"I don't know, either." I glanced at a trio of teenage girls who passed by. They acted brash and bratty, mirroring what I used to do, flaunting themselves to a group of boys watching them. It made me worry for the girls and distrust the boys. "Have you stayed friends with any of your other lovers?"

"No." He frowned. "Have you?"

I shook my head. "It doesn't sound like the odds are in our favor."

"Yeah, probably not."

It wasn't feasible, anyway, I decided, since we were both supposed to move on with our lives and not look back. Me, in particular, I realized, with my wifely pangs to settle down.

He turned toward the ocean again. I did, too. Someone was playing music now. A live performer, banging a drum. It was getting dark, and people were getting rowdy.

"Do you remember when I wanted to pierce your eyebrow?" Spencer asked, still watching the sea.

It was a strange conversation for him to start, but I went with it. "Yes, I remember." It had been toward the beginning of our Tinder hookup, maybe just a few days in.

"Why did you want to do it?"

"It was just one of those rebellious things, I guess. Piercing someone else."

We faced each other, the drumming getting louder, like heartbeats on the shore, rising with the waves.

"Why did you refuse?" he asked.

"Honestly? I've always been scared of needles."

He smiled a little. "I wouldn't have hurt you, not if I could've helped it."

I returned his smile, enchanted by how he was looking at me. His eyes were black against the backdrop of the sky. But they were always dark, always compelling. "Don't even think of trying to talk me into it now."

"Which one was I trying to convince you to pierce?"

I pointed to the left. "It's a little less arched than the other side."

He kissed the brow in question, making my pulse flutter. He was good at being gentle. He excelled at being sensual, too. Whatever he did pleased and excited me. And for now, I was going keep him as close as I could.

Until I couldn't keep him anymore.

We ordered breakfast from room service, and the dining room table in our bungalow was laden with food. Neither of us wanted to cook, and by now most of our groceries had run out, anyway. We would be flying home tomorrow, our trip coming to a close.

While we ate, I thought about all of the touristy things Spencer and I had done. One of my favorite places was Griffith Observatory. Not only was the hilltop view specular, portions of *Rebel Without a Cause* had been filmed there. Yep, the location where James Dean had worn his iconic red jacket. Fashion was everything to me, especially with how hard I'd worked to become a stylist. If I lived in LA, I would probably be dressing movie-industry people instead of country music personalities, like in Nashville.

"What do you want to do today?" Spencer asked. "Any ideas of where you'd like to go?"

I opted for something personal. "You can take me to your old high school." I explained my interest in it by saying, "I'm curious to see where you misspent your youth."

He cocked his head. "As opposed to where you misspent yours?"

"I went to a public school with overcrowded classes and overworked teachers. And besides earning a slutty reputation and having my name written on various walls and desks, I was always in detention with the other misfits."

"Spending your Saturdays in the library?"

"Not quite." I crinkled my nose. "Our punishment was picking up trash in the yard, like some sort of prison road crew."

He lifted his brows. "What was the nature of your crimes?"

"Mostly I got into trouble for mouthing off to my teachers." I'd always had an aversion to authority.

An amused look appeared on his face. "Now, why am I not surprised?" The amusement faded when he said, "I attended a private academy. Rigid, disciplined. The kind that's supposed to keep its students in line."

I watched him cut into his pancakes. "I'll bet you found plenty of ways to break the rules."

"I got suspended a few times. But they never expelled me. I was a bit of an enigma back then. A troubled kid who always made the honor roll. As messed up as I was, I was still a good student."

"Not me. I was lucky that I graduated and finally buckled down in college." I tasted my eggs Florentine. We'd gotten separate entrees, but we were sharing a fresh fruit platter and a basket of muffins. "Can we go to your old school? I just want to see the outside of it." I didn't expect to wander the halls with him.

"If you insist. But it's just a big stuffy campus with rich kids in preppy uniforms."

"I still want to see it."

"All right, but please don't ask me to drive by my aunt and uncle's place."

"I would never do that." I knew better than to subject him to revisiting the home he'd hated. "Besides, it's a gated community, isn't it?"

"I still know people in that area, and I could get in if I wanted to. But I prefer being locked out." He blew out a noisy breath. "I keep hearing that you're supposed to forgive the people who hurt you. Not for them, but for yourself. But it's not easy, letting the pain go."

"That's how I feel about Kirby."

"Yes, but Kirby wants to repair the damage he

caused." He softened his voice. "You're like family to him, Alice. You should give him a chance."

I tensed, my spine going stiff. "He's not my family."

"He could be if you'd let him."

"Why? Because he's related to my sister's husband? Your aunt is family and look how awful she was to you."

"My aunt doesn't give a crap about me. But Kirby cares about you, more than you realize."

"I'm so sick of you taking his side." I got up to leave the table, stomping over to the living room.

Spencer followed me. "I'm sorry if I upset you."

I glared at him, standing my ground. "Why can't you take my side for once?"

"And why can't you accept that Kirby cares about you?"

I scoffed, and he reached for me, ever so gently, ever so warm. He had a knack for doing that. I tried to wriggle away from him, but he wouldn't let me go. I shivered, hating the effect he had on me.

Hating it. Loving it. Feeling confused by it.

"You can't be all nice now," I said. "It isn't fair."

"I'm just trying to do the right thing."

"And making me want you." In spite of how angry I was, I caressed his face, skimming the back of my hand along his beard stubble. It was impossible not to touch him.

He leaned forward. "Now who's making who want who?"

I pulled him closer, rubbing my body against his.

I played with his hair, wondering how it would look if he grew it long.

We stripped each other bare and stumbled into bed, almost as if as we were drunk on each other. It wasn't a reference I should've used, but it was the only one that came to mind. As I moaned and sighed, he traced my temporary tattoo, peppering my skin with warm, wet kisses.

He used his tongue between my legs, and I gripped the sheet, tugging on the material, eager to come. I knew it wouldn't take long. I was already losing my sense of reason. I closed my eyes, going hot and damp.

Suddenly I couldn't remember anyone else ever making me this aroused. Only him. I climaxed, making throaty sounds, bucking against his face.

I opened my eyes and saw that strong, handsome face. I reached out to trace the sharp edges of his cheekbones.

We switched places, and I used my mouth on him, giving him the same intimate pleasure that he'd just given me. He stopped me before I went too far, even if his muscles were quavering, even if I could've taken him all the way.

I took charge of the condom, rolling it over every big, hard inch. He groaned and entered me, pushing deep inside. I clasped my legs around him, squeezing tight.

I didn't want to go home tomorrow. Or maybe I just didn't want to go back to living alone. I liked sharing this space with him, sleeping beside him each night and waking up with him each morning.

But I had to stop thinking about things like that. Once we were back in Nashville, I couldn't let him matter so much.

My plan didn't work. We'd been back in Nashville for a month now, and the more time I spent with Spencer, the more important he became. I was knee-deep in our affair and protecting my heart, too. By now, I was beginning to want more. But his feelings hadn't changed, not as far as I could tell.

On this sunny afternoon, I arrived at his house, with a stack of copies of the magazine he was featured in. I'd gone downtown to get them, to an old brick-and-mortar bookstore. I had a digital copy on my iPad, but I wanted hard copies, too.

I rang the bell, but he didn't answer. I tried the door and found it unlocked. He'd obviously left it that way for me.

I set down the magazines and called his name. He didn't respond, so I searched for him. Finally, I spotted him in the backyard with Cookie and Candy, playing fetch with them. It made me wonder if he would be good with kids, too.

Not that I should care, I told myself. Spencer wasn't going to be the father of my children. At some point, our affair would be over.

I went outside to greet him, and the dogs dashed over to me. They wagged their tails, rolling over at my feet. I scooped both of them up and nuzzled their furry heads.

Spencer watched me, and I leaned over and embraced him, with the dogs between us. He laughed when one of them pawed at his shirt. They were his babies. For now, they were mine, too. But someday, I still wanted the human variety.

I released the dogs and said, "I got the magazine. I bought all of the copies they had."

"I don't understand why you want so many of them."

"Because I have a crush on you." I fanned my face, pretending to swoon, even if the feeling was real. "Let's go look at it together."

He ducked his head, embarrassed by my enthusiasm. "I've already seen it, Alice."

"You saw the digital version. You haven't seen the glossy pages. You look even sexier that way."

He cringed, but it only endeared him to me that much more. He seemed boyish today, chuffing like a kid.

"That's all I need," he said. "To ogle myself."

"Come on." I tugged him inside, leading him into the living room, where I'd left the magazines on the coffee table.

The dogs accompanied us, jumping onto the sofa to see what the fuss was about.

"Check this out, girls." I opened one of the copies to Spencer's layout. "The new heartthrob in town." I turned to a photo of him perched on his motorcycle, where he'd been looking off camera at me. "This is my favorite."

Cookie sniffed the picture, and Spencer groaned. He could deny his sex-symbol status all he wanted, but his Instagram had blown up since the magazine came out. He already had tons of female followers, but as of yesterday, his fan base had practically doubled. I'd also picked up new followers, simply from being associated with him. He'd definitely been right about that. Having a hot lover was making me popular. Luckily, I'd gotten work out of everything, too. Derek had referred me to some important jobs. The work I'd done for Spencer was changing my life.

"He's a reformed bad boy," I said to the dogs. "See, it says so right here."

Cookie sniffed the magazine again, and I bumped Spencer's shoulder, teasing him. But deep down, I couldn't bear to think about the next woman who was going to share his bed.

Why couldn't he be the right man? Why couldn't he be my future? I ached that I wasn't allowed to love him, that I had to fight my feelings.

"Kirby called me this morning," he said.

I closed the magazine with a frustrated snap. Kirby was the last person I wanted to discuss.

Spencer continued by saying, "He's planning a get-together at his house, and he invited us. It's going to be a family party, with his kids and grandkids and whatnot."

I frowned. "Mary didn't say anything about it."

"He hasn't spoken to anyone else about it yet. He wanted to check with me first."

"Why? What's going on?"

"Nothing, except he's hoping I'll finally give in and meet his family." He met my squinting gaze. "I said that I'd go if you did."

I debated my options. On one hand, I worried that I was being railroaded into this. But on the other, I thought that Spencer needed more family-type ties. Why? I asked myself. Because I wanted him to become a family man himself? Either way, at least I would get a chance to see how well he got along with children. For all I knew, fatherhood might actually be in his future someday.

I could hope…couldn't I? That maybe he could morph into my Mr. Right. That eventually he might start having the same types of feelings for me that I was having for him.

I said, "We should accept the invitation."

"Really?" He pushed his hair away from his forehead. "I expected you to put up more of an argument or refuse to go at all."

"I think it'll be nice for you to bond with Kirby's family. They're the best part of him." Especially my niece and nephew, I thought. My sister and Brandon, too.

He cleared his throat. "There are other things about him that are admirable."

"If you say so." Which he did, over and over, like a broken record, annoying me to no end. "When is this party, anyway?"

"He hasn't set a date yet. But I'll let him know that we're on board."

"Are you nervous about it?" I couldn't tell by his expression.

"A little, I guess." He leaned in my direction. "But it should be easier having you there."

"I'm only going to support you. I'm not doing this for Kirby." I leaned toward him, too. "But for now, why don't you take me out to the garage and ravish me on your Harley, like the hot guy in the magazine would do?"

"Come on, Alice, that guy isn't real."

"He is to me." I put my hand on his thigh, creeping toward his fly, letting him know that I was serious about what I'd said.

"Damn." His eyes glazed over, and his body went taut.

I sucked my bottom lip between my teeth. I was opening his zipper now. "I thought you might see it my way."

"You're very persuasive. But let's do this right." He scooped me up, carrying me in his arms. A man on a passionate mission.

He stopped to get a condom out of the bedroom, tossing me onto the bed while he secured it in his pocket. He picked me up again, and I clung to his embrace.

He balanced me, shifting me in his arms, and headed down the hall. He went through the laundry room and pushed open the garage door. With everything we'd done in the past, we'd never messed around on his Harley.

"This might not be very comfortable," he said. "For either of us."

"I don't care."

"Neither do I." He set me down and peeled off my panties, draping them from one of the handlebar grips.

I wore a loose dress, making it easy to straddle the machine. He climbed in front of me, and we kissed, wet and rough, slick and hard.

A moment later I said, "When I started having fantasies about being with you again, I was worried that you were going to make me reckless, like I used to be."

"That's not what I'm doing. You're still going to marry Mr. Right and have a respectable life."

I was having a tough time picturing that now, not unless he turned out to be that man.

I felt Spencer's hand moving under my dress. I gasped and lifted my bottom off the seat.

"Just a bit of foreplay," he whispered.

I glanced down and saw that his jeans were still undone. "Can I touch you, too?"

"Not yet." He continued his sexual foray. "I want you to come first."

I leaned back, giving myself over to him in every way I could. Except for loving him, I thought.

I was still too afraid to do that.

Eleven

Spencer

I sat on a padded stool in Kirby's studio, my booted heels pressed against the footrail, and thought about Alice. We'd gotten down and dirty in my garage less than twenty-four hours ago, and now she was on my mind again. I couldn't go a day without craving her. But it wasn't just the sex. It was other things, too: the warmth, the friendship, the closeness we'd come to share. I was starting to have feelings for her that scared me.

Bonding-type stuff.

Maybe even love-type stuff.

Kirby sought my gaze, and I did my damnedest to relax. He'd invited me over to listen to some new tracks, but we hadn't done that yet. We were talking about the party instead.

"Alice agreed to be there for sure?" he asked, seeking to confirm what I'd already told him in a text.

"Yes." I made another attempt to relax. I was just a guy in recovery, trying to keep his head on straight. What did I know about love?

Nothing, I thought. But it was okay; I didn't need to freak out. Sooner or later, I would stop seeing Alice, and then these scary feelings would go away.

Kirby blew out his breath. "I really hope this gathering will make her feel more comfortable around me."

I understood his reasoning. He wanted to create a sense of home and hearth, drawing her into the fold. "I know how important this is to you, but maybe you better not get your hopes up too high."

"At least it gives me a chance to see her. The only other times I'm able to do that is at the twins' birthday parties, and she ignores me at those functions."

"She might ignore you at this one, too." I wasn't trying to be negative, but I hadn't seen any signs of Alice softening toward him.

"Maybe it'll be all right if you're there, guiding her through it. I can't tell you how glad I am that you're going to meet my family. I know how you long you've been avoiding these kinds of situations."

I'd gotten used to being a lone wolf. And now I was putting myself in a position of being part of a pack. I was also waiting for the results of the DNA test I'd submitted on the ancestry sites to find my own father and see if there was a familial match. My world was spinning. But so was Kirby's. We both had a zillion things on our minds.

"Maybe you should do it soon after the party," I said.

"You mean tell Alice that I might be her dad?"

I nodded, and he rubbed a hand across his beard. He looked old and tired. Worried, it seemed, about how she was going to react when the time came. Would she learn to love him, to accept him? Or would she hate him even more? I prayed it wasn't the latter.

After a bout of anxiety-ridden silence, I said, "Maybe she'll be ready to hear it by then. And even if she isn't, we can't drag this out forever."

"Has it been hard on you, keeping my secret?"

"Everything just seems like it's getting more difficult." Sleeping with her. Lying to her. Getting close to her. "I never expected to have this kind of affair with her."

Kirby squinted, making the lines around his eyes more pronounced. "Are you falling in love with her, son?"

Damn, I thought. Did he have to go and say that? I glanced around, looking for an escape. The walls were closing in.

"Spencer?" He prodded me.

I gripped the undersides of my chair, my knuckles going as white as the ink on my tattoo. "I don't know." I stared at him, needing his guidance, his wisdom. "What does it feel like to fall in love?"

He came closer to where I was, grabbing a stool for himself and placing it next to mine. "I think it's a little different for everyone, depending on their situation. When I first fell in love with my ex-wife, I thought I'd be with her forever, considering how open our marriage seemed. But it got tense later, and I hurt her by having a child with another woman."

"Did you love any of your mistresses?"

"I loved Matt's mom, but that relationship went awry, too. I'm not a good example of how a man in love should behave. I was too selfish to give someone else what they needed."

"What about now?" I asked. "Are you better at it with your girlfriend?"

"Yes, but I'm not consumed with being in a relationship and neither is she. It's a different dynamic. Calmer, more mature."

I was consumed with Alice, but did that mean that I loved her? "I'm confused about how I feel."

"I understand that you're struggling to come to terms with your feelings. But you're a good man with a good heart, and I'd be thrilled for you and Alice to stay together."

"Thanks for your confidence. But I'm not right for her." I wasn't Alice's dream man. Was I? At this point, everything seemed chaotic.

"Maybe you should ask her how she feels. She might be confused, too."

It was sound advice, but could I do it? Not now, I decided, not this soon. "It might be too much to throw at her, with everything else that's going on. I think it would be smarter to wait."

"All right. I'll call my boys and set a date for the

family gathering, and you just try to breathe easy. Okay?"

"You, too." He still looked worried about how Alice was going to react to his news.

We were both stressed over the same woman, but for different reasons. And I feared it was only going to get worse before it got better. If it got better at all.

Two days later, Alice asked me to spend the night at her place. But I probably should've stayed home. I was in a lousy mood. Just that morning, I'd learned that there were no matches for my DNA. No hits whatsoever. It made me feel more alone than ever.

I waited to tell her until bedtime, and she reacted with empathy in her eyes.

"Did you get the results from both websites today?"

I nodded. "Neither of them panned out. No distant cousins. Nothing."

"I'm sorry."

"It's okay." I gazed at the TV mounted on her wall. We were streaming *Sons of Anarchy*, the way we'd done at my house on the day of the photo shoot.

She muted the sound. "No, it isn't. I can tell how disappointed you are."

"I didn't really expect it to be that easy. To just submit my DNA and magically find my dad or someone from his family."

"I know. But you still had hope that maybe it would work."

I shrugged. I was all screwed up. Not just about

whoever my dad was, but about how Alice was making me feel, too.

Was I falling in love with her? Was that happening to me?

She rolled over, skimming her hand along my tattooed arm. The temporary one from LA was long gone. I missed seeing it on her skin, knowing that I'd put it there.

"I can help you," she said.

I glanced up. "What?"

"To find your dad."

"How?" I asked, becoming suddenly aware of her silky white nightgown. She rarely wore those sorts of garments to bed. It made her look like a bride. Or my vision of one.

I frowned at my own idiocy. Weddings were the last thing that should be crowding my already cluttered mind.

"We could contact a private investigator and give them whatever information you have."

"I hardly have any info. And I don't want to get a PI involved." It just felt too personal to me, handing my family history over to someone else.

"Then we can do it ourselves. We can talk to your mother's old friends, the ones she was traveling with when she met your dad. They might remember something useful."

"I have no idea who took that trip with her. Besides, I haven't seen any of her friends since she died."

"Do you know any of their last names?"

"I remember Joanie Pierce. She was an aspiring actress back then. She's the one Mom called to take her to the hospital, who was with her when she passed." When my life had been blown apart, I thought.

Alice touched my arm again, softly, comfortingly. "Then we can start there. We can do this together."

I reached for her, more confused than ever. She was offering to help me find my father, and I was withholding information about hers and panicking about falling in love with her.

"Maybe we should wait a while," I said. "I don't think I'm ready to continue my search just yet." I couldn't go on a daddy quest, not now, not like this.

"Just let me know when you're ready." She nuzzled against me. "I'll be here for you, Spencer."

Overwrought with anxiety, I held her. But in the pit of my screwed-up soul, I wanted to run and hide. To bow out of Kirby's get-together. To not search for my father. And most of all, to stop seeing Alice. Yet as overwhelmed as I was, I couldn't seem to let her go.

She said, "I hope that when you're ready, we're able to find your dad or someone from his family. Ever since I reached out to my dad's family and connected with them online, it's brought me some comfort."

Her attachment to Joel's family wasn't going to help matters, not with the likelihood of Kirby being her father. But for now, I needed a reprieve, not just from our dads, but from my jumbled feelings for her.

I moved away from her and gestured to the TV, where crimes were being committed. "Do you want to finish watching the show?"

"Okay." She reached for the remote.

She unmuted the volume, and I let the noise engulf me.

I appreciated the diversion, until the scene changed, showcasing a painfully tender moment between star-crossed lovers.

I suffered through it for a while, but when it dragged on longer than I could bear, I said, "Maybe we should turn it off now."

"But we just started watching it again."

I made a face. The couple on the screen were locked in an emotional embrace. "It's getting late, and I think we should get some sleep."

She checked the time on her phone. "It's not even eleven."

I defended myself. "I've been up since really early, and it's been a long day."

She conceded. "You're right. I'm sorry." She pressed the off button on the remote. "We can finish it another time."

I motioned for her to extinguish the light. The lamp was on her side of the bed.

She darkened the room, and we closed our eyes and spooned. But sleep didn't come easy for me. I stayed awake, pressed against her. And as I listened to her breathe, as I kept her unbearably close, my angst intensified.

Right along with my fear of love.

I woke up the next day, feeling exactly the same way. Alice wasn't beside me anymore. She'd gotten up and left me alone.

I searched for my phone and checked the time. I'd slept until noon. I dragged my ass into the shower and soaped down.

Afterward, I got dressed and found Alice in the living room, curled up on the couch, with her nose buried in her laptop. Was she shopping for one of her new clients? I should be working, too, composing at my piano. But I was here instead, staring longingly at her.

She glanced up and spotted me. "Hey, sleepyhead."

"Afternoon," I replied, hiding my emotions.

"Are you hungry? You missed breakfast, but I made pasta salad for lunch. There's a bowl of fresh melon, too. I already ate, but it's in the fridge if you want some."

"I wouldn't mind a few bites." Some fuel to restore my brainpower. I went into the kitchen and got the food.

I came back and sat next to Alice, watching her out of the corner of my eye.

She closed her laptop and said, "You had a tough night."

At least I hadn't been plagued with one of my nightmares. That would have left me in a sickening sweat. "Did I wake you with my tossing and turning?"

"Yes. But I fell back asleep. Were you stressing about what we talked about? About finding your father?"

"I guess so." I couldn't admit that I was frazzled about my feelings for her. Or that I was keeping a secret about her family.

"Too bad people weren't doing selfies back then. If they were, your mom probably would have snapped one with your dad."

I put my plate down. "Do you have pictures of your parents you can show me?" I was especially curious to see her mother—the woman Kirby had swept into two troubling affairs.

"I have some separate ones of them in here." Alice reopened her laptop. "I just need to find them."

She had tons of current photos. I peered over her shoulder, watching as she scrolled through them. Her sister and the kids were in a lot of them. Her BFF Tracy, too.

"Oh. Here's my dad." She opened it to full view.

I analyzed Joel. He had a lanky build, sandy blond hair and a casual demeanor, the exact opposite of Kirby's rugged appearance and outlaw persona. Alice didn't resemble Joel. She didn't look like Kirby, either. I couldn't begin to guess which of the two men was her father.

"He seems like he would have been a nice guy." I felt bad that her mother had cheated on him, but he was gone now. Kirby was still alive, worrying that Alice might be his daughter.

"His family says great things about him." She clicked to the next picture. "This is Mama, before she got so depressed."

Cathy had refined features, framed by dark red hair tumbling past her shoulders. She posed playfully for the camera, radiating innocence, sprinkled with a dash of sex appeal. Were those the qualities she'd conveyed when Kirby had first come upon her?

"She's so pretty." So intriguing, I thought. "You favor her." Except Alice looked much wilder.

"Do you have any pictures of your mom I can see?"

I nodded. "Most of them are in boxes in my attic, but I scanned a few onto my phone." I removed it from my pocket and opened the file. Up until now, I'd kept the album private. Alice would be the first person to view it. Rather than narrate, I handed her my phone.

She studied the first image, a headshot from my mother's portfolio, showcasing her long, wavy brown hair, expressive eyes and glittering smile.

"Oh, Spencer. I can see her being an actress. She probably could've modeled, too. She was a natural beauty." Alice lifted her gaze. "You don't look like her, though. Even with as handsome as you are, you don't have any features in common with hers."

Clearly, I favored my unknown dad. "My aunt used to say that I inherited my mom's spirit." Of course, coming from her, it hadn't been a compliment. But to me, it was.

Alice continued going through the album. "Is this you?" She grinned at the screen.

I leaned over to see what it was. "Yep. Yours truly." I was about five, dressed in a fireman's costume, the red plastic hat practically wobbling on my head. "I wanted to be a firefighter back then."

"You were adorable."

"I was shy."

"And now you're all grown up." She roamed her

gaze over me. "Big and strong and sexy. You can put out my fire anytime."

I stared back at her, admiring the way her stretchy little top clung to her breasts. "I think I'd rather ignite it."

The sound of a text interrupted our flirtation.

She returned my phone to me, without glancing down at it. I appreciated her respecting my privacy.

I checked the notification. "It's from Kirby. He said that he can do the party this Saturday. I guess everyone else is available then. Is that too soon for you?"

She sighed. "It's fine."

"It's okay with me, too." I wanted to get it over with, the sooner the better. "I'll let him know."

"I'm excited about you meeting the twins." She scooted closer to me. "You like kids, don't you?"

"I haven't been around that many. But yeah, I like them. Children and animals make the world go around." When she smiled, I skimmed her cheek. But before I touched her too much, I said, "I should go. I have to work."

"Me, too, actually. But we'll see each other on Saturday."

I got up and carried my barely touched food into the kitchen. I'd gotten too sidetracked to eat.

She walked me to the front door and kissed me goodbye, her lips tenderly fusing to mine. I slipped my arms around her waist and examined my feelings for her once again. Yet I left without getting anything resolved.

I was still as confused as ever.

Twelve

Alice

I rode with Spencer to Kirby's party. I wasn't thrilled about socializing with Kirby, but I was determined to get through it. I wanted Spencer to get comfortable in family settings, and that was worth having to cross paths with Kirby.

We stopped at the security gate, and the guard let us in. Kirby's house was an elaborate Southern mansion, renovated to fit his needs.

We parked in the circular driveway. We weren't the first to arrive. In fact, it looked as if everyone else was already there.

Sure enough, they were. The family were gathered outside on the patio, a huge entertainment area flanked by grass and a playground for the grandkids.

I spotted Hailey and Hudson on the swing set with their cousin, Zoe, who was Tommy's six-year-old daughter. Tommy was the middle Talbot son and a country superstar like his dad. He used to have a playboy reputation; groupies went wild for his messy-haired, hazel-eyed, daredevil charm. He was happily married now, and Sophie, his lovely brunette wife, was pregnant with their second child. I'd heard it was a girl, due sometime next month.

They were the first to greet us and make Spencer's acquaintance. When Sophie waddled over and initiated a hug, her big beautiful belly bumped against me. It gave me a warm feeling, and I imagined the babies I hoped to have one day.

The men shook hands, and Spencer congratulated Tommy on his new reality show. The first one Tommy had done was so successful, the network had created another one exclusively for him. He liked working in television because it kept him home with his family instead of out on the road touring.

I looked around for Kirby, but I didn't see our host anywhere. I spotted Mary organizing the dessert table with pastries she'd baked. She never showed up any-where empty-handed. Brandon was by her side, help-ing her. Kirby's chef and his staff stocked the main buffet, getting it ready, too.

Soon Mary and Brandon made their way over to us, and I introduced them to Spencer. I'd told Mary that my romance with him wasn't serious, but I wasn't

sure if she believed it now that she'd had the opportunity to see us together. Maybe she could tell that
I was fighting my feelings for him. Or maybe I was
just so consumed with it myself, it felt obvious to me.

The final Talbot brother, Matt, and his wife, Libby,
approached us. They lived on a recreational ranch in
the Texas Hill Country with their three sons. Their
oldest boy, a thirteen-year-old named Chance, was
Libby's son from a previous marriage. Sadly, her first
husband had died. She'd gotten to know Matt while
she was researching the biography Kirby had hired
her to write.

I watched Matt and Spencer converse. It was interesting to see them together, these two mixed-blood
men. As far as I knew, Spencer didn't socialize with
any other Native Americans. He didn't attend tribal
gatherings; no powwows or drum circles. Maybe that
would change if he ever met his father or got to know
that side of his family.

I decided to inquire about Kirby. It seemed odd
that he was absent. "Where's your dad?" I asked Matt.

He replied, "In the barn with my boys."

"Chance wanted to take his little brothers to see
the horses," Libby interjected. "And Kirby went with
them."

"That's nice," I said. I meant about the kids seeing
the horses. But I let Libby draw her own conclusions.

She nodded and smiled. She was a perky blonde
with peekaboo dimples. I had no idea what she saw
in Kirby, but she adored him, along with the other
women who'd married his sons—my sister included.

Kirby finally showed up, strolling back from the barn in his custom cowboy gear. Matt and Libby's sons dashed ahead of him and joined the rest of the kids in the play area. Chance carried his youngest brother piggyback style, the little boy clinging happily to his neck. At Chance's age, I was already running wild and getting into trouble.

Kirby acknowledged Spencer, and they embraced.

Kirby turned to hug me, and I went stiff. He embraced me, anyway. "I'm so happy you accepted my invitation," he said. "Thank you for coming."

"I'm here for Spencer," I replied.

"I know." Kirby smiled. "He's a great guy. It's nice that you two…" He fumbled a little, then said, "You get prettier every time I see you, Alice."

I could feel Spencer watching us, and it made me feel even more awkward around Kirby. Normally I did whatever I could to avoid him. Admittedly, though, we'd worked well together on Tracy's album when Kirby had used me as consultant on my mother's music. But there had been plenty of tension, too, with me snapping at Kirby whenever things didn't go my way.

Was I being too hard on him after all of these years? Should I try harder to forgive him?

I glanced over at Matt, thinking about what he'd overcome. He'd forgiven Kirby for abandoning him when he was young. He'd found the strength to let his pain and anger go. From my understanding, he'd done it for his wife and children, not wanting to raise his family from a place of resentment and hate.

If I had a family of my own, would this be easier for me? I moved closer to Spencer, realizing full well that he was the man I wanted to marry.

The man I loved.

As difficult as it was, it was foolish to keep fighting it. Yet there was no turning back now that I'd admitted it. I had no choice but to accept my feelings. Nonetheless, my heart knocked against my rib cage.

"I'm going to check on the kids," I said. I needed an excuse to be alone, to calm the palpitations.

I walked away, forcing my legs to carry me. Spencer remained with Kirby. I could tell that as two recovering addicts, they really understood each other.

Did I understand Spencer? Would I make him a good wife? I shook my head, realizing how foolish my inner dialogue was. Spencer and I weren't headed down the aisle.

But if we did get married, in my fantasies, anyway, I might consider getting closer to Kirby. Not for myself, but for Spencer. I couldn't go around hating his mentor.

I plunked down on the grass, released the air in my lungs and observed the kids. In addition to the swings, their playground consisted of a bouncy castle, a slide and a roundabout. I used to love those when I was little. I would hold the handles and run as fast as I could, then jump back on and spin. I didn't need to do that now. I was already dizzy from my thoughts.

I stayed by myself for a while, immersed in the activity around me. By now, parents were calling their children, gathering them for lunch.

Spencer came over to me, and I gazed up at him, my breath catching at the familiar sight of him. If only I could tell him that I loved him.

"Are you okay?" he asked.

"I'm fine." I shined the spotlight on him. "How about you? Are you having a good time? Are you connecting with Kirby's sons?"

He nodded and crouched beside me. "I really like Matt. He's so down to earth, so real. I like Brandon and Tommy, too. I'm glad I'm getting to know everyone."

"I think you fit right in." He already seemed as if he was part of this group. "I'm glad we came."

"You are? For sure?"

"Yes. I might even try to say a few words to Kirby." Maybe it wouldn't hurt to make a teeny bit of effort, just in case Spencer and I actually became a bona fide couple someday.

"Oh, Alice, that would be great. He was hoping that we would sit at his table." He motioned to the buffet. "Should we get our food?"

I agreed, and we filled our plates with picnic-style entrees and colorful side dishes. I loaded up on fried chicken and potato salad. Spencer took extra helpings of the barbecued ribs, messy as they were.

Kirby's girlfriend, Debra, arrived, running late from work. Tall and trim with graying blond hair and a professional sense of style, she certainly seemed nice enough. But Kirby always surrounded himself with goodhearted women.

I chatted with her about inconsequential things. I

made small talk with Kirby, too, even if it pained me to do so. Whenever he looked at me, I thought about the anguish he'd caused my mother: the nightly tears, the daily despair.

My teeny bit of effort wasn't the least bit effective. I was angry at him all over again.

After we ate, I asked Spencer to sit on the lawn with me. I needed to get away from Kirby and try to relax.

Hailey and Hudson wandered over to us, and I smiled, eager for Spencer to engage with them. Except that the kids were quiet for now. Hudson was being his usual reserved self, and Hailey kept glancing over her shoulder, probably waiting for her cousin Zoe to join us. The last I saw, Zoe had spilled a cherry-filled, chocolate-covered dessert on her blouse and was getting cleaned up.

Matt's boys had gone back to the barn. Hudson could've hung out with them, but he stayed with his sister instead. He'd always been fiercely loyal to her, even before they could walk or talk. I assumed it was a twin thing and the time they'd spent together in the womb, just the two of them, preparing to enter this big, bad, crazy world.

Zoe came running up with a damp spot on her top, and soon she and Hailey were holding hands and swinging their arms back and forth. Rather than be left out, Hudson crawled onto my lap. I nuzzled the top of his silky head. The girls, however, stared blatantly at Spencer.

"Hey, ladies," he said, and made them giggle.

Zoe sized him up, her long, brown ponytail swishing as she bobbed her head. Then she looked at me and asked, "Is he your boyfriend?"

Her question made my heart jump. I sucked in my breath and debated how I should respond. I glanced at Spencer, but he didn't give me any indication of what to say.

"Yes, he is," I finally replied. Maybe it was the dreamer in me, but calling him that made me feel deliriously good.

Zoe shifted her attention back to Spencer. "Are you her boyfriend because you kiss her?" She nudged Hailey, and my mischievous niece puckered her lips and made smooching sounds.

I struggled not to laugh. I envisioned the two of them creating all sorts of chaos when they got older. They'd certainly poked some childish fun at me and my "boyfriend."

He furrowed his brow. "I don't think we should be talking about this."

"Why not?" Zoe was an outspoken first-grader, determined to get a straight answer out of him. And on top of that, Hailey was still making kissy noises.

"Because we just shouldn't." When both girls frowned at him, he seemed to be searching for something to say that would distract them. He settled on, "Did you know that I have lots of dogs?"

"How many?" Zoe asked, taking the bait.

He told the kids about his rescue, and Hudson chimed in and babbled about Cline, the husky his dad had named after country crooner Patsy Cline. Only

Hudson referred to her as "Patty." Spencer grinned, amused by the boy's mistake.

The boyfriend topic was forgotten. But not by me. It gave me hope, feeding my dream of having a future with the man I loved.

The party ended, and Spencer and I returned to my house. But when he entered my condo, he fell silent.

I removed my shoes and sat on the sofa, looking up at him. "Is something wrong?" He was acting strange.

"I don't know. There's just a lot…" He hesitated. "I just…"

"You just what?" My heart sank. Was he concerned about me calling him my boyfriend? Was it bothering him now? Was he getting ready to break things off? Would this be our last night together? I waited for him to say what was on his mind.

He finally responded, "I have feelings for you that confuse me. You and I weren't supposed to be getting this close." He remained standing, watching me through troubled eyes. "I'm not the guy you're meant to be with, but I…"

I released the breath I'd been holding, hope spiraling inside me. "Do you want to be with me?"

"Sort of. I think so. I don't know." He sat beside me, with the late-day sun streaming through the blinds and creating a sudden glare. I squinted, and he shifted his body to shield me from the light. After a moment of us just staring at each other, he said, "I don't want to mess up your plans. Or disappoint you."

"You could never disappoint me. Not unless you

stopped seeing me. Not unless you went away." I wanted to tell him that I loved him, but I was afraid to say it this quickly.

He reached for my hand. "Does that mean you want us to try to make a go of this?"

"Yes." I wanted everything with him.

"Are you sure? Because we both know that I'm still coming to grips with who I am. I don't ever want to drink again, but what if I screw up? Resisting the temptation isn't as easy as I keep saying it was."

"I already knew you were exaggerating that. Or I assumed you were. I didn't think it could be that easy."

"Sometimes it keeps me up at night. I have hideous nightmares about it."

I squeezed his hand. "I read a study about dreams once, and it said that nightmares were a normal reaction to stress and can even help people work through their fears."

"Yeah, but what if I can't handle the pressure?"

"Of your nightmares?"

"Of me and you."

I tried not to panic. "Of being my boyfriend?"

"Of loving you, Alice." His voice turned shaky. "I think I might be falling in love with you."

To be sure I'd heard him correctly, I repeated it. "You think you *might* love me?" It wasn't exactly a vow of forever, but, by heavens, it was a start. "That's what you said, right?"

"Yes, but what do I know? I've never been in love before."

Nether had I, not until I'd fallen for him. "I don't blame you for being scared. It's all so new and different." I'd already struggled with it myself.

"I'm not freaking you out?"

"No." Hearing him say that he "might" love me gave me comfort. I looked into his eyes. "I tried to fight it. But I love you, Spencer. I absolutely do."

He blinked at me. "You trust that I'm the guy you want?"

I nodded. I had no reason to distrust my feelings. "I know how important your recovery is, and how hard you work at it. I think that you'll stay sober." I needed to believe in him, to support him, to help him overcome his fears. "But if you ever slip up, you'll have me to catch you when you fall."

"That's a huge commitment."

"It's what people in love do."

He frowned. "I hope you don't change your mind later."

I stuck to my guns, clinging to my belief in him, the way a caring partner was supposed to do. "I won't."

"You could." He spoke gently. "I want to protect you. I want to keep you safe."

"I already feel safe with you." I couldn't imagine not having him in my life. Alice in Spencerland. I smiled at the thought. It was a place I never wanted to leave.

"I wasn't prepared to be having this conversation with you, to be talking about love. Not with everything else that's going on."

"What do you mean?"

"I can't get into the details right now. I wish I could, but I can't."

Was he keeping a secret about himself? Was there more to his past than I knew about? I tried not to worry. "Is it something bad?"

"It might seem that way at first, but it doesn't have to be. It can actually be something good, if you let it." He trailed a finger across my cheek. "I just want you to be happy and accept whatever is meant to be."

I leaned into his touch. Now he was being mysterious. But if he thought his news bordered on good, then I would wait to hear what it was. I didn't want to destroy the moment. I needed this closeness with him.

He kissed me, lightly on the lips. Then he said, "I swear, I'm only trying to do what's right. But I hope you understand that I need to talk to Kirby about it first."

I fought the urge to flinch. I hadn't expected Kirby to be part of Spencer's secret. Or whatever this was. But given how tight they were, I shouldn't have been surprised that he'd involved his mentor. "If that's what you need to do, I'm not going to stand in your way."

"Thank you for trusting me."

I refused to let Kirby spoil my belief in Spencer. "I'm supposed to trust you, especially now that you're my boyfriend."

He laughed a little nervously. "The kids sure teased us on that one. But I think I can do this without being so afraid."

"You'll have to write a song about it, asking yourself 'Do I love her? Am I in love?'"

"Is that how the answer will come?" He fixed his gaze on me. "Is that how I'll know for sure?"

"Maybe," I said, hoping he found a way to unscramble his feelings. In spite of him saying that he was less afraid, he still seemed scared.

On Monday afternoon, Spencer called and told me he wanted to disclose the secret he'd been keeping. I still couldn't fathom what it could be, but I was glad he wasn't dragging it out. Nonetheless, he'd warned me that Kirby was going to be there, too. I wasn't happy about that, but it seemed important to Spencer to have his mentor in the mix.

Anxious, I got ready to go. I did my hair and makeup and slipped on a trendy jumpsuit, fitted with a high neck and long sleeves. The weather was on the cooler side.

I arrived at Spencer's place and spotted Kirby's luxury SUV in the driveway. I dreaded seeing Kirby, but at least I was supporting Spencer. My lover was waiting for me on the porch. He smiled and greeted me.

"You look nice," he said, reaching for my hand.

"Thank you." We went inside, and as we entered the living room, I glanced past him and spotted Kirby on the sofa. He jumped up as soon as he saw me.

Suddenly, I sensed that this wasn't going to go in my favor. I was beginning to feel like an outsider, particularly with the looks the men were exchanging.

"What's going on?" I asked.

"Kirby's needs to talk to you," Spencer replied.

I frowned. "About what?"

His breath hitched. "The secret I've been keeping for him."

Spencer's secret was Kirby's secret? I didn't like the sound of that.

"Maybe you should sit down," Kirby replied. "Because we... I have a lot to tell you."

"I'd prefer to stand." They were both standing, too, with Spencer's shiny red piano in the background.

He gently asked me, "Can I get you anything?"

"No." I didn't want a soft drink or whatever he was offering. I just wanted to hear what his mentor had to say. I clutched the chain strap on my purse, pulling it tighter against my shoulder.

"Try to keep an open mind," Spencer said. "And please, give Kirby a chance."

I zeroed in on the older man. He shifted his weight, moving from one foot to the other.

"A chance at what?" I asked him.

He replied, "To be your father. I think I might be your dad, honey."

I stared at him, unblinking, unmoving. Was I going into shock? Nothing made any sense. "That's impossible. I was eleven years old when you met my mom."

"I knew her before then. I had an affair with her about nine months before you were born. But I never told anyone about that affair, and neither did she." He reached into his pocket and removed a crumpled envelope. "I have a letter that your mom wrote to me during that time."

My blood roiled in my body, in my heart. My breath stuck in my throat. I was too livid to look at Spencer. I kept my focus on Kirby, on the enemy. "Did she tell you that I might be yours? Is that what's in the letter?"

"No. The only reason I wanted to show it to you is because of when it's dated."

"A date that proves you might be my dad?" That he'd slept with her nine months before I came along? I felt queasy now, dizzy and sick. I didn't want Kirby to be my father. I wanted Joel to be my daddy. The man my mother was supposed to have loved.

"I suspected that you might be mine on the day I first met you. I took one look at you and felt an over-whelming connection. But I couldn't be sure, so I kept my feelings to myself. Then, earlier this year, I came across the letter and all of the pieces seemed to fit."

I locked my knees to keep them from buckling. "How long has Spencer known about this?" I still couldn't bring myself to look at him.

"I told him right after you two started seeing each other again."

"I'm sorry," Spencer interjected. "But I couldn't tell you about it, Alice, not without betraying Kirby's confidence. It needed to come from him."

I didn't care what his excuse was. He'd known the whole time we were lovers, and that wasn't fair. I'd never felt so betrayed. I ached so badly, I wanted to scream.

Kirby said, "I'm hoping that you'll agree to take a paternity test. In my heart, I believe that you're mine. But I want for both of us to know for sure."

Was he kidding? There was no frigging way I was submitting my DNA for him. "You're not my father."

"I think I am," he countered softly.

I shook my head. I couldn't let him be my dad. I just couldn't. "If you were, my mother would have told me."

"Maybe she didn't know for certain herself. Or maybe she knew and just couldn't face it. With the way I seduced her, she hardly stood a chance. She was a sweet lady, and she deserved better."

"You're despicable." I hated him more now than I ever did.

"I know, and I'm sorry for hurting your mama the way I did. But I've been trying to right my wrongs." He clutched the letter that was still in his hand. "I really want us to be family."

"Family?" I shot back. "Give me a break." I hated him, but now I hated my mother, too, for her part in the lie. Was there anyone I could trust? Anyone who'd been truthful? I finally looked at Spencer, with his dark eyes and strong-boned features, with his tall, tanned body and white tattoo. "As for you, *my boyfriend, my lover*." I mocked those words. "I never want to see you again." Before I collapsed into tears, I turned on my heel and headed for the door.

I rushed outside and accidentally dropped my purse, the contents spilling out of it and littering Spencer's porch.

"Alice." I heard his voice from behind me. He'd followed me out.

I was already on the ground, trying to gather my belongings. He knelt to help me.

"Don't," I said, firing my pain at him. "Just don't."

He didn't listen. He stayed there, insisting on helping me. My things were everywhere. I grabbed my lipstick before it rolled off the porch and into the dirt.

"I'm so sorry." He handed me my wallet, his voice turning raw. "I never meant to cause you harm."

I started to reject his apology, but he kept talking.

"Kirby didn't tell you right away because he was concerned about what your reaction would be. He asked me to help him get closer to you, and he left it up to me, as to when I thought you'd be ready to hear it. I didn't know what to do. But after I started having deeper feelings for you, I thought the time was right. I wanted to make everything better, to get it out in the open. I swear, I only had your best interest at heart." He paused, with his voice still raw. "When I was doing the DNA search for my dad, I kept thinking how strange it was. Me looking for my father, when Kirby could possibly be yours. I know how hard this is for you, but I think it would benefit you to know the truth, to take the test to see if he's your dad."

My pain and anger intensified, his explanation falling on deaf ears. I tersely said, "You conspired with him the entire time you were with me." I shoved my wallet back into my bag. "I should have known better than to trust you."

"I was just trying to bring the two of you together.

And then later, I was trying to figure things out with you and me, too." He rocked forward on his knees. "Please, don't leave. Don't go."

I pushed his hand away when he tried to reach for my compact. "Why? Because you *might* love me? Sort of like Kirby *might* be my dad." I scoffed at both scenarios.

He watched me, his face shadowed, his eyes hooded. "I can't help how confused I've been. But don't give up on us."

"Us? There is no us anymore." I couldn't bear to be needed by him or wanted by him or anything that involved his disjointed feelings for me. "I can't be with you."

I crammed the rest of my belongings into my purse. I didn't know if I was Kirby's daughter. I didn't know anything, except that deep in my battered heart, where it hurt the most, I still loved Spencer.

And for me, that was the most devastating part of all.

Thirteen

Spencer

I watched Alice leave, hating what I'd done to her. I hated myself, too. These past two years of self-exploration had just turned to self-loathing. I'd hurt the woman I loved.

The minute she was gone, I recognized my feelings, understanding them fully. I was desperately, hopelessly in love with Alice McKenzie. But I couldn't jump on my Harley and chase after her. How hypocritical would that be? I couldn't return to the house and write a song about love and redemption, either. This wasn't one of my bullshit compositions, garnering praise and winning awards. This was my reality, my failure, and even my music seemed like a farce now.

I'd kept a secret from her that I shouldn't have kept. Mr. Right wouldn't have made a mistake like that. He would've known the difference.

Kirby came outside and approached me. There was a moment of silent reflection between us.

I spoke first. "I lost her. She's gone."

"I'm so sorry," he replied quietly, shamefully. "This is my fault."

"No. It's mine." I wasn't going to let him take responsibility for my actions. "I could've refused to keep your secret."

"And I should've left you out of it altogether. I involved you in something that put you in a difficult situation. I created a hardship for you and Alice." He leaned against the porch rail. "It's obvious that you love her."

"It doesn't matter."

"That isn't true. She needs you."

"What? You're the authority on love now?" I gave him a frustrated look. "The last time we talked about love, you said you weren't the best person to give advice."

"I'm not. But I know love when I see it."

"That doesn't mean I can make it work. What she needs is the man she's been dreaming about. And I'm not him."

"I think you are."

I wasn't going to listen to him. His judgment about me was clouded. Alice had seen the true me: the jerk who'd hurt her. "She deserves better than what I can give her."

"She deserves to know how you feel."

"No, she doesn't." By now, I was craving a drink. God help me, but I wanted to belt down a quick, hard shot.

I turned away from him, afraid that he would read the craving in my eyes. Intent on keeping my expression steady, I stared out at the arbor embellishing the walkway.

But instead of falling silent, I said, "Did I tell you that she offered to help me search for my dad?" I barked out a cynical laugh. "While I was withholding information about who her father might be, she wanted to unite me with mine."

"You were only trying to protect her. To keep my secret until the time was right to tell her."

"Yeah, and look how that turned out. Not just for Alice and me, but for you, too." I released a rattling breath. "I'm sorry she refused to take the DNA test."

"She has a lot to deal with."

"More than enough." She'd chosen to end it with me, and I could hardly blame her. All I could think about was the bar in my living room, beckoning me, offering to numb the pain.

I kept staring at the arbor, focusing on the vines creeping up and around the woodwork. I sensed Kirby studying my profile. Was he analyzing me?

"Maybe you should come home with me, son."

No way, I thought. No effing way. I didn't want

him being my watchdog. I turned toward him again, as if I had nothing to hide.

"Thanks for caring," I said, trying to sound grateful, the way I'd always been in the past. "But I really need some time alone."

He squinted suspiciously at me. "You're not going to do anything stupid, are you?"

"Of course not." I wasn't going to admit that I was on the edge of destruction. I had to make Kirby believe that I had myself under control. After what had just happened with Alice, I didn't want to involve him any deeper than he was already was. Or maybe I just wanted an excuse to fall off the wagon. Either way, I couldn't handle being around him right now.

He grabbed my shoulders, almost as if he meant to shake my disease out of me. "Are you sure I can trust you?"

"Absolutely," I lied through my teeth. "I just need some space." I turned the tables on him. "What about you? Are you going to be all right?"

"I'll be fine." He squeezed my shoulders. "I really wish you'd come home with me."

"I understand your concern." I preyed on his kindness, telling him what he needed to hear. "I'm not naïve. I know how something like this could affect my sobriety. That I could freak out once I'm alone." I looked him straight in the eye, determined to seem strong and true, as honest as a broken man could be. "But I swear, I'll call you if I get even the slightest urge to drink."

He released his hold on me. "Promise?"

"Yes," I lied again, anxious for him to leave me alone with my pain. Because, really, what difference did it make? Whether I got drunk or strayed sober, Alice would still be gone.

And I would still be missing her.

As soon as Kirby got in his SUV and drove away, I paced my living room with my eye on the bar. I hunted it like a vulture, getting closer to the drink I craved.

On the night Alice and I first hooked up, I'd poured rum over us in the shower, dousing our naked bodies with it. Was that the liquor I should have now?

Hell, yes, I thought.

I uncapped a bottle of Bacardi and inhaled it, remembering how intoxicating it had smelled on Alice's skin—like oak and molasses, heady and sweet.

Maybe I could guzzle half of it and take a sloppy bath with the rest. I could keep my clothes on if I wanted to, drenching them, too. I could do whatever absurd thing I felt like doing. There was no one here to stop me. No prying eyes. Not even the dogs. I'd taken them to the rescue earlier.

Squeezing my eyes shut, I took another desperate whiff, my hands quaking, my breathing coming in short, addictive bursts. I couldn't help but think how good the rum was going to taste, how buzzed I would get, how much I wanted it.

I sank to the floor, clutching the bottle, debating, with a sickening feeling in my gut, whether or not to take a drink.

I opened my eyes, shame coiling inside me. Was this what I'd reduced myself to? A liar? A cheat? A coward? A pitiful drunk, feeling sorry for himself?

I caught my reflection in the glass panels on the bottom of the bar, and my shame deepened.

I didn't do it. I didn't let the alcohol pass my lips. I didn't bathe in it, either. I got up off the floor and recapped the bottle, returning it to the bar. But I was still shaking, still trying to catch my breath.

Now what? I asked myself. What was my next brilliant move?

The answer knocked against the walls inside my brain. I knew exactly what to do. I got my phone and called Kirby.

He answered on the second ring. "Spencer?"

"Yeah, it's me." He already knew who it was, obviously. My name would've appeared on his screen. "I lied to you earlier. I was having terrible urges when you left here. But I managed to get through it."

"Oh, thank God." His breath rushed out. "Do you want to come to my house now?"

"I'd rather stay here." In the place I called home, I thought. "But I need to attend a meeting." To share my feelings with the group, to admit that I'd almost relapsed, using the woman I loved as an excuse to crack open a bottle.

"The next meeting isn't for a few hours."

"I know." We both had the schedule memorized. "But if you want to hang out with me until then, that'll be okay."

"I'll be right over." Relief sounded in his voice.

"I'm so glad you called me. Should we dismantle your bar when I get there? Pour all of that temptation down the sink?"

"No." I stated my case. "It's imperative for me resist it on my own, not remove it from the equation. Besides, I can't pretend that it doesn't exist."

"That's not what I'm asking you to do."

"Yeah, but that's what getting rid of it would feel like to me."

"All right. We'll do it your way. I'll see you soon."

"Okay."

As I waited for Kirby, my house seemed eerily quiet. I decided to bring the dogs home. I had time before Kirby arrived to get them. I grabbed a jacket and left through the back door, taking in the crisp Tennessee air.

It felt good to walk, but I was still overcome with emotion. I needed to write a song for Alice, telling her how sorry I was, telling her that I loved her. I was wrong about my music being bullshit. My work was an extension of myself, the good and the bad, the light, the dark, the man, the musician, the recovering alcoholic.

I didn't know if she would ever forgive me. But I wanted her to know how I felt about her. She was my heart, my soul. As clichéd as that sounded, it was true.

I couldn't erase the affair Kirby had had with her mother or take away the possibility that he might be her dad. I wasn't a miracle worker. I was just a guy who loved her.

I had no idea how long it would take for me to create a song like that. A few days? A few weeks? The rest of my life? I couldn't attest to anything anymore, except how much she meant to me.

I made it to the rescue and found Cookie and Candy in one of the fenced yards, playing with Pete. The three of them ran over to me, and I knelt to greet them. Pete nudged me, and the girls danced in happy circles, looking like dust mops. I smiled at the memory of Alice calling them that. I missed her so much, I could barely breathe.

I didn't want it to be over, but the choice didn't belong to me. Once I offered her my heart, she would have to decide what to do with it. For now, all I could do was pray that I hadn't lost her for good.

I didn't go straight home after the meeting. I headed to a neighborhood rife with specialty shops. I had a compulsion to buy a loose black diamond, a stone to remind me of Alice. A talisman, I thought, something to bring me luck.

There was only one jewelry store, a quaint little place near a music shop I frequented. I liked the vibe of this part of town.

I entered the jewelry store and approached the front counter. An older man glanced up from beneath his glasses. He resembled Albert Einstein, with his electric white hair. I imagined him having the perfect stone, just waiting for me.

I told him what I wanted, and he furrowed his bushy white eyebrows. My hope waned. His reaction didn't strike me as positive.

"I only have one black diamond," he said. "And I just set it in a piece this morning."

"If I buy it, can you remove it from the setting?" I was determined to make this work in my favor. I didn't want to leave empty-handed. Or empty-hearted, I thought.

"Sure, I could do that. But maybe you better take a look at it. It's over five carats and is a rare stone. I'm not trying to lose a sale, but it's a pricey piece of jewelry."

"I'm not concerned about that." I would spend whatever was necessary to have a stone and have it today. I'd already talked myself into thinking I needed it.

He looked me over, probably thinking I was crazy. Maybe I was. But I didn't care. I was hell-bent on leaving here with my talisman.

"It's over this way." He came out from behind the counter and led me to a small glass case.

I spotted the diamond before he pointed it out, and my heart slammed to the back of my throat. It was set in a woman's ring. A solitaire. Just the stone and a shiny gold band.

"It's an emerald cut," he said.

I didn't know one style from another, but the diamond was a rectangular shape. The color was opaque, denser than I would've expected. Yet it still seemed magical. I leaned over the case, staring at it through the glass.

"Most black diamonds on the market are man-made," he said.

"But this isn't?"

"No. It's completely natural and untreated."

I was mesmerized. Not only by the diamond, but by the ring itself. Now I wanted to buy it for Alice, which made no sense. There was no guarantee that I would win her back. Or that the song I was going to write would even reach her ears. She might refuse to listen to anything I had to say.

But I still had to try. I wasn't going to mention how close I'd come to relapsing in the song. That needed to be said in person, face to face, eye to eye, if I ever got the opportunity to talk to her again.

"Is it an engagement ring?" I asked.

"That's what I designed it to be." He unlocked the case and removed it, turning the price tag in my direction.

The cost didn't deter me. I held the ring in my hand, feeling its energy. "I heard that black diamonds represent strength and power."

"That's true. They do. But they also represent relationships that are destined to prevail, no matter what the odds."

Now I knew, absolutely knew, I was making the right decision. I loved Alice enough to devote myself to her, to try to be the man she needed. So why not ask her to marry me, if it was possible? A humble proposal, I thought, fraught with hope.

"I want it," I said. "But don't remove the stone from the setting. Keep the ring intact."

"That's a wise choice." He studied me. "Wise, indeed."

Did he suspect that I was lost and trying to find my way? Could he tell that I was aching over an estranged lover? Or how desperate I was to win her back?

We returned to the front counter, and I gave him a credit card for the purchase.

He put the ring in a velvet box and said, "This is some of my finest work. Natural black diamonds can be difficult to cut. That's part of why they command a higher price. I could've easily fractured it."

"But you didn't." And now the ring was in my possession. A symbol of strength and power and defying the odds.

But would Alice give me a chance? Or did I have too many strikes against me to repair the damage I'd done?

Fourteen

Alice

I spent several distraught hours alone in my condo, trying to escape the pain. I wanted to crawl into a deep, dark cavernous hole and never come out. But when the solitude became too much to bear, I called Tracy and my sister, asking them to come over.

After they settled in, the three of us gathered at my dining room table. I sipped the chamomile tea Mary had brewed and relayed my story.

"Oh, no," was all Tracy could seem to manage. She looked stunned beyond words.

Mary, however, slipped into repair mode. I recognized the fix-it need in her eyes. It was her nature to try to hold everything and everyone together. She hadn't been able to cure Mama's depression, though. Our mother should have gotten professional help for that.

"Would it be so bad to have Kirby as your father?" Mary asked. "It's obvious how much he cares about you. Plus, you'd have Brandon, Tommy and Matt as your big brothers, and their kids would be your nieces and nephews. You'd have a whole new family." She paused. "You should agree to take the DNA test. You should try to embrace this, no matter how it turns out."

I gaped at her. "Don't you even care that Mama cheated on Daddy? That she lied to us and told us she only had one affair with Kirby?"

"It concerns me, yes. Absolutely. But what's the point of being angry about it now? Mama is gone. We can't be mad at her over it. That'll only make things worse."

Easy for her to say, I thought, with her perfect life. "You're not the one whose paternity is in question." She hadn't been betrayed by the man she loved, either. I still couldn't believe that Spencer had kept Kirby's secret the entire time we were lovers. "If Kirby is my dad, then what? Am I just supposed to forget about Joel and his family?"

"Of course not. This isn't a case of you shunning Joel's family or not keeping him close to your heart. He's my dad, too."

"He's your dad for certain," I reminded her.

Mary sighed. "I get that you're hurting. And I know you're devastated about Spencer's involvement in it, too. But I think he really was trying to protect you."

"I don't want to be in love with him anymore." I glanced at Tracy, drawing empathy from her. She knew what it was like to be left in shambles by someone she loved.

"I'm sorry this is happening to you," Mary said, interrupting my sad exchange of looks with Tracy. "After everything you went through when we were kids, you deserve to be happy." She heaved another sigh. "I can't do much about Spencer. But do you want me to kick Kirby's ass for you?"

I knew she was joking, but I appreciated her saying it, anyway. "Thanks, but you care about him too much to do that." He'd even walked her down the aisle at her wedding. "He should be your dad, not mine."

"Oh, sure." She cringed. "And how creepy would that be? Me married to his son?"

"That might be a bit of problem." I found the will to laugh. But mostly I was just trying to keep from crying. Kirby was the last person on earth I wanted as a parent.

I finished my tea, and Mary popped up to refill it. She probably would've baked my favorite raspberry cookies if the ingredients were available.

"What are you going to do?" she asked.

"About the DNA test?" I shredded the cover of a fashion magazine I'd left on the table, tearing it bit by bit. "I can't even think about that right now. I can't deal with any of this, least of all what Spencer did to me. I was so careful when I first started sleeping with him, doing whatever I could not to get attached."

Mary put the teapot down. "You can't help who you love."

"And he doesn't even love me back."

My sister frowned. "How do you know he doesn't?"

"He never said that he did, not even when I called him out on it."

Tracy caught my gaze. "Would you get back together with him if he said it?"

"I don't know if there's anything he could say or do that would make a difference now." I piled up the shorn paper. "He didn't just keep an important secret from me. He broke my trust, my heart."

Ripping me clean apart.

I cried myself to sleep that night, and the next morning I got up, needing to get away from Nashville. I texted Mary and Tracy and told them I was leaving town for a few days and not to worry about me.

But where should I go? I considered flying to LA and staying at the Chateau, but that would only remind me of Spencer.

I opted for Oklahoma City, returning to the place where I grew up and where my youthful rebellion had begun. I wasn't sure what, if anything, that was going to accomplish. But it was where my fractured heart was taking me.

I got myself together and packed a bag, preparing for a long drive. On a good day, it would take about ten hours.

And this wasn't a good day.

I took breaks along the way, stopping to eat and use public restrooms. By the time I made it, it was pitch dark, and I was exhausted. I checked into a motel with an old-fashioned neon sign, a gimmicky illusion of simpler times.

My room was adequate: a full-size bed, a standard nightstand, a faux wood table and a generic TV. I could've gone to a luxury hotel, but I liked the privacy this offbeat motel provided.

I showered, using the mini soap, and went to bed in wrinkled pajamas. I was far from the fashionista I normally was.

I slept fitfully, pushing the covers away, then pulling them back up. Nonetheless, I awakened early and decided on fast food for breakfast.

The mopey teenager behind the counter kept stealing glances at the world outside her job, and I was tempted to tell her to appreciate her youth and not throw it away like I'd done. But I doubted that she was interested in hearing what a lonely twenty-five-year-old had to say.

I sat by a window, with a dismal view of the parking lot, and picked at a ham-and-egg sandwich.

Two cups of coffee later, I drove to the park where Mary and I had sprinkled Mama's ashes. It pained me to hate my mother, especially with how vehemently I'd loved her in the past.

I exited my car and walked down a bumpy path, heading for the enormous oak we'd chosen as Mama's unofficial marker.

I found it, tall and strong, amid a grouping of smaller trees. Thankfully, there was no one in this section of the park except for me. I stood at the base of the tree, its branches spiraling above my head.

Was Mama's spirit here?

"Why did you keep so many secrets?" I asked her in a soft and shaky voice.

I waited for her to defend herself. But there was no answer. Not even a leaf blowing at my feet.

"And what about Kirby?" I went on to say. "Is he my father? He seems to think that he is."

Once again, there was nothing, no insight into Mama's side of the story. Clearly, this was getting me nowhere. But I kept waiting for a sign. A hope, a glimmer. Something that proved she was listening.

I dropped down in the dirt and drew flowery pictures with a stick. I even glanced up at the sky and looked for heavenly shapes in the clouds. But no ghostly stirrings materialized, no mother-daughter comfort.

I should've called it quits and left the park. Instead, I told her about Spencer. I talked and talked, revealing how deeply he affected me. I'd never shared these sorts of feelings with her before. But there'd never been a boy worth mentioning until now. Of course, Spencer wasn't a boy. He was the man I'd mistakenly fallen in love with.

I paused, then said, "Spencer and Kirby are really close. They're extremely loyal to each other. But it's so confusing, with how hurt and angry I am." I glanced up at the sky again, frustrated that I couldn't feel her presence.

Still, I prattled on. "Kirby said that he's sorry for everything he did. He even took responsibility for seducing you. And get this—he wants to be my dad. He seems to want it more than anything." I sighed to myself. "Maybe I need to take that DNA test. Maybe knowing the truth will make it easier."

But could I do it without Spencer? I put my hand in my pocket and clutched my phone. Should I call him? Should I confide in him? Or would that be too painful?

"Tell me what to do, Mama," I said, still talking to my dead mother and getting no answers.

Was I wrong, the way I'd left Spencer, with no concern for his feelings or well-being? I'd told him that I loved him, but what kind of love was that?

Did I owe him an apology for getting so angry, for blaming him for everything that went wrong? I hadn't given him time to come to terms with his feelings. I'd chastised him for his fear and confusion, instead of letting him work through it. Maybe if I'd stayed there with him, if we'd…

Just as I prepared to call him, my phone vibrated against my hand. I checked the notifications and discovered a text from Spencer with a video attached.

Oh, my God.

I watched the video, my heart quaking, my pulse skittering. He'd written a song for me, a haunting ballad, and taped himself singing it at his piano.

I played it, over and over. The music was soft and compelling, the lyrics honest and tender. I found it beautifully romantic, but laced with angst, too. A man struggling to find his way back to the woman he loved and asking for her forgiveness.

He'd titled it "Spencer in Love."

I was wrong when I'd told Tracy that I didn't know if Spencer could say or do anything that would make a difference to me now. His song was a reflection of who he was, of how he felt, of how much he loved and needed me.

Just as I loved and needed him.

I peered up at the sky one last time. Maybe Mama was here after all, guiding me toward my future.

I called Spencer, and we raced through an emotional conversation, our hearts beating much too fast. We needed to talk calmly in person. He offered to come to me, saying that he would book the first available flight, whether it be a private jet or commercial airline. Then tomorrow, we could drive back to Nashville together.

We ended the call, and I heard from him again a short time later. He couldn't get a flight as soon as he'd hoped. He wouldn't be here until tonight.

I headed to the mall and shopped for a new outfit to wear, then spent the rest of the day cooped up in my motel, thinking about how it was going to feel to see him.

Evening finally rolled around, and I sat on the edge

of the bed, awaiting his arrival. He was due any moment. He'd texted me from his Lyft.

A knock sounded, and I jumped up.

I opened the door, and there he was, all six feet two inches of him, dressed in a leather jacket and his usual torn jeans. Yet in spite of his familiarity, he seemed different. When I searched his gaze, I noticed a nervous flicker in his eyes. But I ignored it. I was anxious, too.

"Alice." He said my name, and I practically fell into his arms.

He wrapped me in his warmth, in the strength of his body, and we stood in the doorway, locked in a desperate embrace. His mouth found mine, and we kissed. I stood on my toes to reach him. He was wearing boots, and I was in ballet-style flats.

We separated, and I led him into the room. Neither of us spoke for a minute. We simply breathed each other in.

Then he said, "You look so pretty. But you always do."

"Thank you." I gestured to my ensemble. "I bought this today." A feminine blouse and a short black miniskirt. "We can go to a nicer place. A hotel, if you prefer."

"I'd rather be here, where you chose to stay." He glanced around, as if he was picturing me alone the night before. "I'm sorry that I put you through so much misery."

"I'm sorry, too, for not giving you time to figure

yourself out." I paused to consider the look in his eyes. He still seemed nervous. Maybe too nervous? It made me wonder if something was wrong.

He removed his jacket and hung it on the back of a dining chair. "I made so many mistakes."

"We both did." I couldn't fault him for his, not when I'd created problems of my own. "I love the song you wrote for me." I'd told him over the phone how incredible it was, but I thought it was important to repeat it. I'd also told him that I'd made peace with my mother at the park, and I was willing to take the DNA test to unmask my paternity.

He released an audible breath. "You were always meant to be my muse, but I never expected to need you so badly."

"I feel the same way about you."

We stared silently at each other, and in spite of the depth of emotion between us, our reunion turned awkward. Something definitely wasn't right.

Unsure of what else to do, I inquired about his mentor. "Does Kirby know you're here? Did you tell him I was in Oklahoma and that you were coming to see me?"

"Yes, I'm keeping him informed." He hesitated. "Are you going to be able to handle it if he's your dad?"

"I'll do the best I can." I didn't want to hold grudges anymore, to keep hating Kirby. I'd spent too many years mired in anger. I didn't know how easy it was going to be, letting go of all that hurt, but I was willing to try. For myself, for Spencer. I was even doing it for my mom. "It's going to be scary taking the test, though."

He nodded. "Waiting for the results will probably be the hardest part."

"I'll definitely be on pins and needles." I studied his solemn expression. "I still want to help you find your dad when you're ready."

"Thank you. That means a lot to me." He tugged a hand through his hair, pushing it away from his forehead. "I need to tell you something that I didn't include in my song."

"Go ahead." At least now I would know what was troubling him.

He frowned. "I almost drank again. When I was alone and missing you, I opened up a bottle of rum, the same brand I played around with on the night we first hooked up."

My heart skipped a worried beat. "But you didn't drink it?"

"No. But I came horribly close."

"Are you still craving a drink?"

"I'm not craving anything except to be with you. But are you sure you want to be with me? Even if I stay on the straight and narrow, even if my nightmares go away, I'll always be a recovering alcoholic. That'll always be in my blood."

I moved closer to him. "I love you, Spencer. All of you. The sober man and the one who almost messed up."

He looked into my eyes, as if he were memorizing

me for all time. "I love you, too. So damned much. But I fell apart when I shouldn't have."

"But you're here now, opening up to me about it." Trusting me with the hardship he'd endured.

"I'm going to do everything in my power not to relapse or let anything like that ever happen again. I want to stay sober for you, for the life I want us to have together. But mostly I have to do it for myself."

"As well you should. But I want to support you." I sat on the corner of the bed and gazed up at him. "Do they have meetings for friends and family members at your recovery center?"

"Yes, and I would love for you to attend them."

I made an earnest vow. "Then I will."

"It feels amazing to love you, to be loved by you. To make promises to each other. But I want to do this right."

"Do what?"

"I'll show you." He walked over to where his jacket was and reached into the pocket, removing a small jewelry box.

My heart nearly stopped. Was it a ring? Was he going to propose? Here, on this very night? It seemed so unexpected, so fast, so exciting. He was making me feel reckless, like he always did. Reckless in love, I thought.

He came over to me and opened the box. It was definitely an engagement ring, a gorgeous emerald-cut black diamond in a yellow gold setting. I gasped like the future bride I was about to become.

He said, "There's a story behind it." He proceeded to tell me how he'd searched for a talisman and had uncovered the ring. "As soon as I saw it, I wanted to buy it for you. But I didn't know if you were going to take me back or if I would ever have the opportunity to give it to you." His dark gaze latched on to mine. "The jeweler who designed it told me that black diamonds mean more than strength and power. They also represent relationships that are destined to prevail against the odds."

"I've never heard that before." But it seemed so right. We were prevailing at this very moment.

He shifted his stance. "I know I'm not the man you dreamed of. I'm not the stuff fairy tales are made of. But I'm going to try to be the best husband possible." He got down on bended knee. "Will you marry me? Will you be my friend and lover for the rest of our lives?"

"Yes." My answer sprang from the deepest part of me, from how much I loved and wanted him.

I leaned forward, and he slipped the ring onto my finger. It was a little big. We smiled knowingly at each other. We were already off to a sweet and candid start.

He sat beside me. "We'll have it sized. But for now, maybe this will work." He yanked some threads from his jeans with a thin piece of denim still attached.

I returned the ring to him, and he wrapped it, as if he was using yarn. I held out my hand, and the diamond went back onto my finger.

He reached for me, and we kissed. It was deep and true, and I felt wonderfully close to this man. I couldn't imagine loving anyone more.

Fifteen

Alice

I gripped Spencer's shoulders, feeling his muscles bunch beneath his shirt. I tugged him down, and we sank onto the bed.

We kissed and kissed, and he asked, "How many babies do you want?"

"As many as we're meant to have," I replied. "But not until after we're married."

"I wasn't suggesting that we start a family now." He smiled. "But someday."

Yes, someday, I thought. I wanted to be the mother of his children. I imagined how perfect they would be, with a combination of our features. "Did you bring anything with you so we can—"

"Make love?" He lifted his wallet from his back pocket, produced a shiny packet, and tossed the leather billfold onto the nightstand.

I pressed against him. "We don't have to take our clothes all the way off." I liked the forbidden feeling of being half-dressed on the night I'd gotten engaged.

I opened my blouse, then removed my panties and rolled my short tight skirt up around my waist. Following my lead, he pulled his T-shirt over his head and shoved down his jeans and boxers.

Sheathed in a condom, he slid between my legs, filling me in one fell swoop. I unhooked my bra, and the garment went slack. He lowered his head to lick my nipples, moving from one side to the other, making me ache.

Pressure built upon need, upon lust, upon love. He breathed in the fragrance of my skin, and I watched him with intensity, welcoming every powerfully driven thrust.

I roamed my hands down the front of his body, heading toward his navel. I accidentally scratched him with my ring, but he didn't seem to mind. I was still getting used to the glorious weight of it.

Soon he withdrew, and we switched positions. I climbed onto his lap and looked down at him—my sexy fiancé, his jeans pushed past his hips, his stomach muscles flexing.

I impaled myself, riding him, slow and slick and wet.

"Do it again," he said. "With the diamond."

I gazed breathlessly at him. He wanted me to scratch him purposely? "Are you sure?"

"Yes." He took my hand and showed me, making the shape of a heart.

I did what he asked. I marked his chest with the stone, not deep enough to scar, but enough to make an impact. A wicked smile appeared on his face, and he lunged forward, stealing a passionate kiss and encouraging me to move faster, increasing the tempo to a mind-dizzying speed.

I don't remember exactly what happened next. Maybe I was too aroused to think straight. But somewhere between the heat and hunger, we both climaxed.

I collapsed on top of him, and he nuzzled the side of my cheek, holding me protectively in his arms.

My lover. My dearest friend. My Spencer.

Upon our return to Nashville, I found a lab that would provide the results of a paternity test within a matter of days. And now that day had come. They were due to arrive by special delivery this afternoon.

I hadn't seen Kirby yet, but Spencer had been communicating with him, acting on my behalf. At the moment, the older man was on his way to my condo. He'd asked if he could be here when I opened the envelope. A copy was being delivered to his house, too, but he wanted us to get the news together. Apparently, he was too anxious to do it alone. I was anxious, too, so I agreed to do it this way and get it over with.

I glanced over at Spencer. He was here for moral

support. Later this week, I would be packing up my belongings and moving in with him. He'd already informed Kirby that we were engaged. I'd told my sister and Tracy, too. Everyone within our circle knew. We'd set the date for six months from now. We were young and eager, and it seemed foolish to wait.

"How are you holding up?" he asked.

"Truthfully? I'm a bit of a wreck." Regardless of the DNA outcome, I'd vowed to forgive Kirby. But what if I couldn't do it? What if all of those angry feelings came flooding back?

"It'll be okay." Spencer came over to me, sitting next to me on the sofa.

He stroked a hand down my back, helping me relax. I turned toward him, and we kissed, the exchange warm and tender, his lips gentle against mine.

Afterward, we looked into each other's eyes, a stream of silence between us. Until the doorbell rang.

"Do you want me to get it?" he asked.

I nodded, my heart picking up speed.

Spencer went to the door, and I could hear him in the entryway, greeting Kirby. I suspected that they were embracing, as they often did.

They came around the corner, to the living room, where I was. Kirby looked fraught with anxiety.

"Hi," I said, rising from the couch.

"Hi," he parroted. "How are you?"

"I'm all right. Just waiting, you know."

"Yeah." He crammed his hands into his pants pockets.

He sported slim black jeans and a black gaberdine shirt with silver piping. His snakeskin boots had Cuban heels and a kerchief tied around one of them. I'd always liked Kirby's over-the-top style, even if I never wanted to admit it.

"Can I get you anything?" I asked.

He shook his head. "No. But I'd love to see your ring."

I approached him and held out my hand.

He let out a low whistle and grinned. "A black diamond? Now that's my kind of jewelry. You're a girl after my own heart."

"I always wanted a black diamond." I smiled at Spencer. "And he gave me one." Five carats and counting. It made quite a statement.

"I'm so happy for the two of you." Kirby sounded like a proud parent.

Was he my father? Was that what the test was going to reveal? I took a moment to analyze my feelings. My hatred hadn't returned. I wasn't consumed with resentment or malice. But did that mean that I'd forgiven him? Or was there still some hurt buried deep inside?

While we waited, I put on some music. The three of us sat, making minor chitchat. It seemed easier than saying anything too personal.

A short time later, the doorbell chimed. I nearly leapt out of my skin. Kirby looked just as antsy.

"I need to answer it," I said. The envelope would be addressed to me, and I would have to sign for it.

As I made my way to the door, I hoped it wasn't

a false alarm, with my neighbor's kid selling cookies or something.

Thankfully, it was a delivery person from the post office. I accepted the envelope from her and returned to the living room.

My palms turned sweaty. "Will you do it?" I asked Spencer. I couldn't seem to manage it.

"Of course." He took the envelope from me.

I turned the music down and glanced at Kirby. He scooted to the edge of his seat.

Spencer opened the results and read them quickly to himself. A second later, he said, "It's not a match. You're not related. Kirby isn't your father." He shifted his gaze to his mentor. "I'm sorry, but she's not your daughter."

Kirby seemed stunned. He barely moved, scarcely breathed. He'd obviously expected a different outcome. I hadn't known what to expect, and now I had mixed emotions.

Joel McKenzie was my father, leaving me with the same DNA I'd always had. But Joel was gone, and Kirby was here, looking sad and dejected.

Oddly enough, I started to cry. For him. For me. For my mother. For all the pain and betrayal over the years.

Spencer came toward me, but I shook my head. I went over to Kirby and cried in his arms instead. He held me, like a father would do, and rocked me back and forth.

I glanced up and saw my fiancé watching us. He understood how badly I needed this. Kirby needed it, too. I was forgiving him, completely, wholly. It didn't matter that he wasn't my father. He was treating me as if I belonged to him.

When I stopped bawling, he handed me the kerchief from around his boot and let me blow my nose on it. I looked up at him, and we both laughed.

A long silence followed, and I thought about Mama and wondered what she would think of all of this. "Will you tell me about when you first met my mother?" I asked Kirby. "I'd like to connect the dots, to try to understand who she was back then."

He winced a little. "It's not a pleasant story."

"I know. But I need to hear it, to make peace with it."

"I understand." He cleared his throat. "I met her at the record store where she worked in Oklahoma. I was there for a promotion, signing CDs and doing a radio interview. She told me that she was working on some songs, but she didn't think they were very good. I encouraged her to keep at it. I even said that someday when she was ready, she could show her songs to me." He made a shamed expression. "She agreed to have dinner with me that night in my hotel room, and one thing led to another. I think she got swept up in my celebrity, in having such a famous man show an interest in her."

"Where was my father all this time?"

"He was out of town on a trucking job. He didn't know anything about where she'd spent the weekend. I remember her telling me that she was in a relationship, and that they had a child together. Your sister would have been around five then, I think."

"Did my mom say anything about my dad?"

"Just that he didn't want to get married. That he didn't believe in it or something. She seemed hurt by that."

"Did she know that you were married at the time and that you had children?"

"Yes, but I told her that I had permission from my wife to sleep with other women, which was true. The only rule was that I wasn't supposed to have kids with anyone else." He shook his head. "But I didn't honor that agreement. I already had Matt by then."

"I have one last question." One more thing I wanted to know about my mother. "What was in the letter Mama wrote to you?" The note with the post-mark that made him think he might've been my father. "What did it say?"

"She was thanking me for encouraging her to believe in her music." He blew out a sigh. "But I took advantage of her when she came back to me, nearly twelve years later, eager for me to hear her songs and hoping that I would buy them. I wasn't her beacon of hope. I was just a self-serving prick who used her, making promises I didn't keep. The worst part was the restraining order I filed, just to get rid of her."

I merely nodded. I couldn't deny that being labeled a stalker had been Mama's biggest downfall.

"I'm not making excuses," he went on to say. "But I was a terrible person then. My substance abuse was out of control, and I was going through women like water. Your mom was just one of many. I blocked her from my mind as time went on, until I pretended that I'd forgotten all about her. But I never really did."

"It's over now," I assured him. "And we both have to stop hurting over it."

"I know, but I'm always going to wish that you were my daughter. I can't help but feel that way."

"We can still learn to be close, spending time to get to know each other. Weekends, holidays, whatever it takes." I offered him a smile. "We can be friends who seem like family."

He smiled, too, his eyes going misty. "I would love that."

This was a milestone for him. And for me, as well. I'd just given Kirby, my old archenemy, a piece of my heart.

I glanced at Spencer. His expression was filled with joy. Clearly, he loved the idea of me bonding with his mentor.

I went over to Spencer and sat beside him. He took my hand and held it. I breathed softly, almost dreamily, just having him near me. A burden had been lifted from my shoulders.

I was finally free of the turmoil that had dictated my life. Free to move forward with the man I loved.

And become his wife.

Epilogue

Spencer

Today was my wedding day, and the ceremony would be taking place at my house, outdoors on the lawn. Alice hadn't allowed me to see her gown yet. I would be viewing it for the first time during her bridal march.

For now, I was in one of my guest rooms, where I'd just put on the designer tux Alice had chosen for me. I stood alone in front of a mirror, thinking about who I was and how far I'd come.

We hadn't located my father yet. I still didn't even know his last name. I might never meet him, and I was okay with that. But we would keep searching, in case he was meant to be found.

As for the wedding, Alice had asked Kirby to walk her down the aisle, which thrilled him to no end. It made me extremely happy, too. I loved seeing them together.

I'd chosen Sam, my alcohol counselor, as my best man, and Tracy, of course, was the maid of honor.

We'd also gotten Kirby's family involved. His sons were my other groomsmen, and his daughters-in-law, including Alice's sister, were the other bridesmaids. The Talbot grandchildren were our flower girls, ring bearer and pages. The youngest granddaughter would be wheeled along in a festively decorated stroller.

Our reception was going to be banging, with Kirby, Tommy and Tracy as the entertainment. The three of them had agreed to perform, each taking the stage at different times. Per Alice's request, Tracy would be singing the songs Alice's mother had written.

I'd included my mom, as well, by wearing a small framed picture of her attached to my boutonniere. Alice had ordered it for me, and it was a beautiful charm and tender keepsake. I know that my mother would've adored Alice.

I took an eager breath and prepared to go to the makeshift altar. Right on time, I made my way to the ceremony, where our guests were already seated.

When the procession started, the bridesmaids and groomsmen walked together, paired in couples.

The kids were next. A couple of the boys walked my dogs. Yep, Candy and Cookie were part of it, wearing rhinestone collars and cute little veils. The doggie duds were Alice's idea. Pete tromped along, too, in a bow tie. The oldest grandson held his leash.

The last boy to appear was Hudson, clutching the ring pillow. The flower girls followed him. Zoe pushed the floral-draped baby stroller, and Hailey scattered glittered rose petals.

Then it happened…

The music changed, and I saw my bride. I watched as she held Kirby's arm and smiled at me. Her long white gown boasted a pearled neckline and a slim black sash, tied elegantly at her waist. Her white-blond hair was spiked, as usual, but the very tips were dyed black. I loved how wild and unconventional it was.

I wanted to break tradition and kiss her as soon as she reached me, but I waited.

Kirby handed her over to me, and I told her how beautiful she looked. She reached up to skim my jaw, and we gazed romantically at each other.

The vows were clean and simple and true. Within no time, we were married. We kissed, and our guests erupted into cheers and claps. Even the dogs barked their approval.

Alice laughed, and I swept her into a playful hug and swung her around. I'd found my lifelong partner, my shining muse, and I was never letting her go.

* * * * *

*Don't miss Tracy's story
as the Daughters of Country
series continues in*
Wild Nashville Ways
by Sheri WhiteFeather!

*Available July 2020
from Harlequin Desire.*

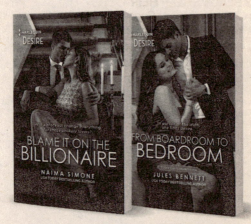

After ending a sizzling summer tryst years ago, marketing VP Max Abbott doesn't anticipate reuniting with Quinn Bazemore—until they're forced together on an important project. He's the last person she wants to see, but the stakes are too high and so is their chemistry...

Read on for a sneak peek at
A Reunion of Rivals *by Reese Ryan.*

"Everyone is here," Max said. "Who are we—"

"I apologize for the delay. I got turned around on my way back from the car."

Max snapped his attention in the direction of the familiar voice. He hadn't heard it in more than a decade, but he would never, *ever* forget it. His mouth went dry, and his heart thudded so loudly inside his chest he was sure his sister could hear it.

"Peaches?" He scanned the brown eyes that stared back at him through narrowed slits.

"Quinn." She was gorgeous, despite the slight flare of her nostrils and the stiff smile that barely got a rise out of her dimples. "Hello, Max."

The "good to see you" was notably absent. But what should he expect? It was his fault they hadn't parted on the best of terms.

Quinn settled into the empty seat beside her grandfather. She handed the old man a worn leather portfolio, then squeezed his arm. The genuine smile that lit her brown eyes and activated those killer dimples was firmly in place again.

He'd been the cause of that magnificent smile nearly every day that summer between his junior and senior years of college when he'd interned at Bazemore Orchards.

"Now that everyone is here, we can discuss the matter at hand."

His father nodded toward his admin, Lianna, and she handed out bound presentations containing much of the info he and Molly had reviewed that morning.

"As you can see, we're here to discuss adding fruit brandies to the King's Finest Distillery lineup. A venture Dad, Max and Zora have been pushing for some time now." Duke nodded in their general direction. "I think the company and the market are in a good place now for us to explore the possibility."

Max should be riveted by the conversation. After all, this project was one he'd been fighting for the past thirty months. Yet it took every ounce of self-control he could muster to keep from blatantly staring at the beautiful woman seated directly across the table from him.

Peaches. Or rather, Quinn Bazemore. Dixon Bazemore's granddaughter. She was more gorgeous than he remembered. Her beautiful brown skin looked silky and smooth.

The simple, gray shift dress she wore did its best to mask her shape. Still, it was obvious her hips and breasts were fuller now than they'd been the last time he'd held her in his arms. The last time he'd seen every square inch of that shimmering brown skin.

Zora elbowed him again and he held back an audible *oomph*.

"What's with you?" she whispered.

"Nothing," he whispered back.

So maybe he wasn't doing such a good job of masking his fascination with Quinn. He'd have to work on the use of his peripheral vision.

Max opened his booklet to the page his father indicated. He was thrilled that the company was ready to give their brandy initiative a try, even if it was just a test run for now.

It was obvious why Mr. Bazemore was there. His farm could provide the fruit for the brandy. But that didn't explain what on earth Quinn Bazemore—his ex—was doing there.

Don't miss what happens next in
A Reunion of Rivals by Reese Ryan.

Available July 2020 wherever
Harlequin Desire books and ebooks are sold.

Harlequin.com

Get 4 FREE REWARDS!

We'll send you 2 FREE Books plus 2 FREE Mystery Gifts.

Harlequin Desire® books transport you to the world of the American elite with juicy plot twists, delicious sensuality and intriguing scandal.

FREE Value Over $20
